Copyright Page

The Shadows Rise © 2026 Joseph L Wiess

For permission requests, write to the publisher at:
Golden Plains Press
JosephWiess@gmail.com

This is a work of fiction. Names, characters, places, and incidents either are the product of the author's imagination or are used fictitiously. Any resemblance to actual persons, living or dead, events, or locales is entirely coincidental.

ISBN:979-8-9957017-3-6

Cover Design: Joseph L Wiess

Edited by: Joseph L White

Printed in the United States of America

To my family: love you all.

To My Substack Subscribers – You're the best.

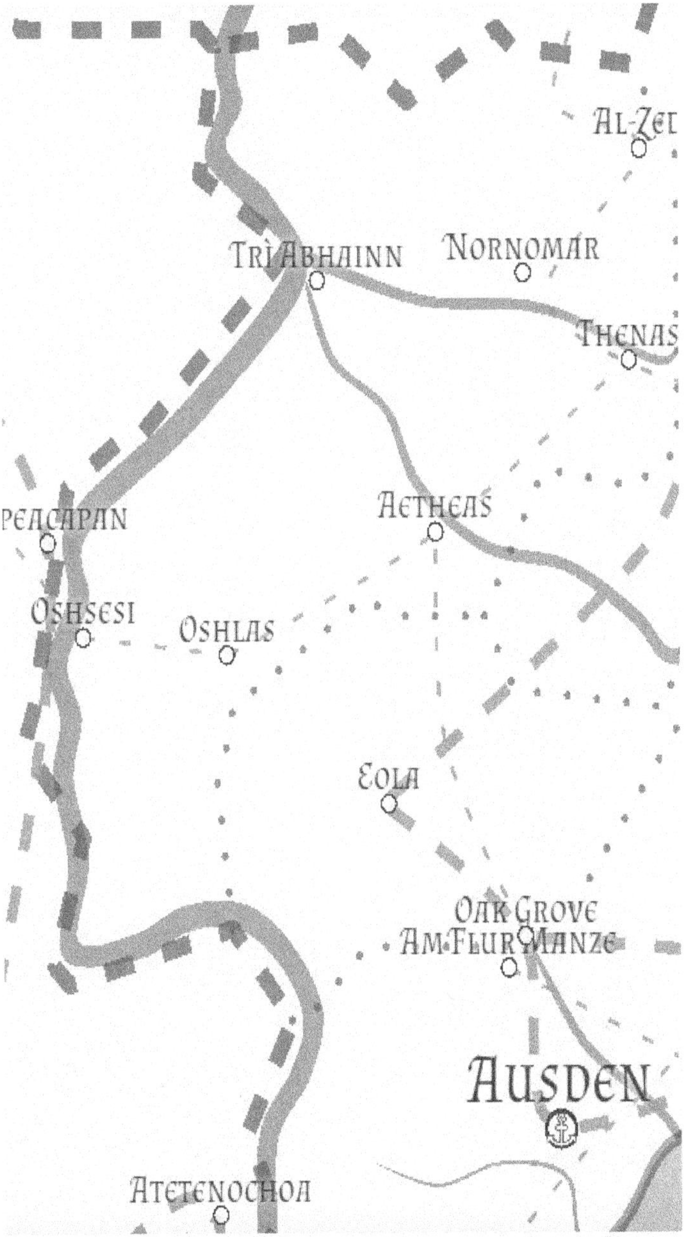

Al-Zet
Tri Abhainn
Nornomar
Thenas
Aetheas
Peacapan
Oshsesi
Oshlas
Eola
Oak Grove
Am Flur Manze
Ausden
Atetenochoa

CHAPTER ONE

The Shadow at the Crossroad

The treacherous magus stood alone at the crossroads where four ancient roads met, one leading into the forests of Astinmah, another toward the frozen hills of the Saorsa, and the others vanishing into wastes long claimed by shadow.

Meron's head was bowed, buried deep within the cowl of his ash-gray cloak. Snow whispered from a bruised sky, drifting in slow, uncertain spirals. None of it dared to settle where he stood. The air itself recoiled.

The world here was hushed, not merely quiet, but listening.

The wind that brushed across the barren plain carried the faint scent of ash and cold iron, and beneath it, something older: the musk of soil that had not been turned in centuries.

Each breath he drew steamed faintly in the air, yet the snow that should have gathered at his feet melted before it touched the ground.

Even in Long Sleep, the necropolis carved deep beneath the mountains north of Saorsa, he had felt it: the tremor that rippled through Crann Na Beatha when Death and Despair, servants of the Spider-God, returned from Iktomi's plane bearing the eggs of the suffron.

He remembered the sound of their hatching: the first breath of darkness splitting stone, the low hum that made even the dead stir. The creatures had spilled forth, half-formed and hungry, eager to crawl into the cracks of the living world.

Their release had been premature. Disorderly. The act of servants, not of their master.

Iktomi himself would never have wasted his children in haste. Chaos, to the Spider-God, was patient and precise, a web spun in stillness, every thread placed with intent.

The magus smiled faintly beneath the hood. In that patience, he was his god's truest reflection, calm, deliberate, quietly devoted to the undoing of others.

He had once studied beneath the Generals and Captains of the Saorsan host, men and women who prized discipline and the sacred balance between freedom and order. They had taught him command and strategy, how to build, how to endure.

He had taken their lessons, every maxim of restraint and honor, and bent them toward a new art.

Order, he had learned, could be sharpened into a weapon. A command, properly spoken, could bind more tightly than any chain. Freedom, misapplied, could birth obedience.

He had watched from the necropolis, smiling as one of the suffron, a thing of smoke and hunger, faced his most hated foe: the High Draoidh, son of that accursed nature goddess, Astinmah.

The image still pleased him: the child of wild creation fleeing from a creature born of cold intention.

He and Iktomi worked in mirrored stillness, god and mortal, each using the other's web to reach farther than they could alone. It was not rebellion that moved Meron, nor obedience, only the conviction that a mortal hand might yet weave more finely than the divine.

He had discovered a new art, a way to bind others without Ananke's chains, without invoking the will of Fate herself. His smile was a thin glimmer of white beneath the hood.

The wind sighed through the crossroads like a breath drawn from the underworld. Frost gathered on the stones around him, each crystal trembling as if afraid to form.

The scent of snow and old earth lingered, mingling with a faint tang of iron, the taste of something about to bleed. The world held its breath.

He waited, hands clasped before him, as the shadows thickened at the edge of the road. Somewhere in that depthless dark, a suffron stirred, a thing of smoke and hunger, without shape until called. He could feel its attention turning toward him, cold and curious.

He waited, eyes closed in meditation, as, in the blink of an eye, darkness descended upon the crossroads. Not a casual darkness, but one born of the black moon, when all light and warmth were drawn from the sky and even sound seemed to hesitate.

Then he felt it: the suffron's mental probing, threads of shadow coiling toward his mind. It was not his own death they showed him, but the pain and ruin of his bonds, the women he had made his own, torn and tormented in the dark.

He wondered, with detached curiosity, how the creature would behave if it ever happened upon those same women, women whose fear had been stripped away. How would it react when faced with the ecstasy that comes from surviving one's deepest terror?

Unmoved, the magus waited as the creature circled him. At last, it halted before him, its form shivering between smoke and flesh.

"Who are you that defies my Pavor Umbrae?"

Good. The creature was curious.

The magus extended his left hand, letting the silver chain slide free until the spider medallion swung gently between his fingers.

"I am a servant of the Spider-God."

So we see.

The magus hid a grin. As he had suspected, they were all one being, fragments of a single mind scattered across the world.

"What do you want, servant of the Spider-God?"

The suffron's tone was wary, but its curiosity had not diminished. It was not stupid, and that meant it could be reasoned with.

"I want to help you grow stronger."

He drew back his hood, revealing dark eyes that reflected no light.

"Your deliverers did you no favors, dropping you here with nothing to feed upon."

The suffron's eyes narrowed.

This much is true. The one of us who found rich hunting ground did not feed to satisfaction. Can you do better, Meron the traitor?

The magus offered a half bow, his arms spread wide.

"Much better," he said. "That I promise."

He met the creature's gaze, his voice soft as silk.

"Can you adjust how you feed? If so, I have such delights for you."

A devious smile touched his lips.

"I give my word — you'll savor it."

But first, they'd need a place out of the sight of the gods. Already he could feel their eyes turning in his direction.

Long Sleep wouldn't do. It was too valuable to risk. He needed a place outside the Saorsa, just as old and hidden, forgotten by both myth and memory.

Something tugged at the edge of his mind, a memory of an ancient barrow deep in the mountains. Few living souls had ever found it. The place was close enough to the Saorsa for him to travel quickly, and if need arose, it could serve as an offering to Iktomi himself.

"If I show you a place, can you take us there?"

The suffron blinked, the spirals and lights dancing on its wings pausing.

We can. What do you propose?

Meron smiled.

"I propose that we gather my followers and your other parts —" he paused for a beat. "and meet at this place."

He felt the suffron draw the location from his thoughts.

"From there, we seek better guidance from the Spider-God himself as to his plans."

The shadow-being shimmered in the dark.

Very well. We will gather your men and your bonds and congregate at the barrow. It paused, spiral eyes searching Meron's mind. ***You will be able to bring the master to us?***

Meron nodded, satisfied.

"I will."

Then so be it.

The suffron wrapped the shadows around them, and the crossroads vanished as they were taken from the world of men.

For a brief moment, the two became one and flung themselves out across the world, a pulse of thought and hunger surging through the veins of creation. The shadows of mountains passed beneath them like dark tides, the breath of the living world rippling faintly against their merged consciousness. Each shared fragments of the other, memory, scent, the taste of fear, the shape of unspoken desire, before the web snapped and they were two once more.

When they separated, they stood before a snow-laden barrow beneath a bruised sky. The mound stretched nearly a mile in circumference, its contours softened by centuries of ice and wind. A great oaken door jutted from the side of the hill, blackened by time, its surface carved with faint spirals now half-buried under frost. The air trembled with age. Even the falling snow seemed to hesitate before the threshold.

The suffron tilted its head, spiraled eyes narrowing to slits of darkness.

This place is very old, it said, its voice like silk dragged across stone. **I sense a powerful hunger inside.**

It turned toward the treacherous magus, it's too-long arms brushing the snow, leaving streaks of shadow that refused to melt.

Did you speak the truth when you said you knew the Master's touch?

Meron's gaze lingered on the door, tracing the withered runes that coiled across its grain like veins beneath a corpse's skin.

"I have not lied to you." His voice carried softly in the cold air, a measured cadence that didn't quite rise to warmth. He remembered the suffron's need for proof; he had been no different once — hungry for signs, for certainty, for power that could be touched.

"Inside, I will prove to you that I am my master's servant."

Very well.

The shadows quivered, then multiplied, spreading across the snow like spilled ink. Where there had been one suffron, now five more appeared, shivering between smoke and flesh.

Behind them, Meron's bonds and thirty-one soldiers stood motionless, silent silhouettes amid the whitening gale. Their breath did not cloud the air; they seemed carved from it.

The six shadow-beings merged briefly into a single writhing mass, then unfolded again, sixfold, identical yet subtly distinct, like reflections in warped glass. The wind stilled. The world listened.

What have you done to these people? the suffron asked. **Like you, they don't feel our pavor-umbrae. We could not feed upon them, not even a minuscule amount.**

Meron smiled, a rare, small thing, thin as the edge of a blade.

"I stripped fear from their minds long ago. The only ones they fear are our Master and I."

The words lingered in the frigid air, and even the suffron's spiraled eyes seemed to tighten, as though tasting something unfamiliar, not fear, but the absence of it.

Meron turned again to the barrow. A faint vibration ran through the ground beneath his boots, and the scent of old soil and rusted iron rose like breath from the mound.

"I think it's time to see what's inside, don't you?"

⁜ ✠ ✪ ✠ ⁜

The bitter cold and falling snow reached beneath cloak and fur, threading through every gap as though the wind itself sought to test their resolve. It curled around armor and flesh, rimming metal in pale frost, stinging exposed skin.

Yet Meron's followers did not flinch. Their faces were masks of stillness, eyes unblinking, each breath measured and silent.

Then, as if the storm realized its futility, the cold withdrew, reluctant, whispering through the grass like a beast slinking away from a greater predator. The air settled into a tense, brittle quiet. Even the snowflakes drifted more cautiously now, falling in slow spirals that refused to touch the magus or his servants.

Meron stood before the door, the weight of centuries pressing against his senses. His breath coiled visibly in the air, wreathing him in faint silver vapor as he studied the wards and weaves etched into the ancient oak and iron. The door was blackened by age, the spiral pattern of its runes glinting faintly beneath a crust of ice.

He could feel the latent pulse of power humming beneath the wood, patient, hungry, and aware.

The suffron was not wrong. There was a powerful hunger inside, ancient but recognizable, a vibration that stirred some buried familiarity within him. The magus furrowed his brow. What slept beyond that door? A sliver of the Spider-God's own essence? Or perhaps an old servant, forgotten when the world was young?

He reached out with gloved fingers, tracing the spiral at its center. The surface was shockingly cold, so cold that it burned, and beneath that chill he felt the faint resistance of something alive. Starting from the center, he began to reverse the spiral, turning against the grain and weft, unwinding the old design.

The wood shuddered under his touch. Lines of faint blue light crawled outward like veins, brushing against ancient wards that flickered weakly before breaking apart. The smell of old ash and rusted iron filled the air, mingled with something older, the scent of opened tombs and forgotten blood.

He could feel the hunger stir again, stronger now, pressing against the barrier as if scenting the warmth of life just beyond its prison. The ground beneath him vibrated faintly, and the wind moaned through the hollows of the mound like a voice learning to speak again.

Meron closed his eyes, his lips moving in silent calculation as his fingers completed the reversed pattern. For a heartbeat, the world held its breath. Then, with a slow and grinding sigh, the traps dissolved, and the oaken door crept open.

The sound was low and icy, a rasp that seemed to drag the warmth out of the air. Beyond the threshold, darkness waited, deep, patient, and expectant.

Before placing his fingers on the ancient door latch, Meron glanced over his shoulder. The snow had nearly stopped. What few flakes still fell drifted soundlessly through the still air, catching in the silver of his cloak before vanishing, unwilling to cling. His followers stood motionless behind him, a phalanx of silence and breathless devotion. Frost glimmered on their armor; their eyes fixed on him alone.

"Touch nothing inside, unless I say so," he said, his voice low but cutting clean through the frozen air. "This place belongs to an ancient power."

His two bonds exchanged a brief nod, small, practiced, precise. Behind them, the soldiers gave no visible sign of acknowledgment, yet their stillness was answer enough. Each of them waited as if carved from the same unyielding ice that surrounded the barrow.

Meron's gaze shifted to the suffron. The six shadows had gathered loosely about his men, their forms half-blurred by the dim light bleeding from the open door. Their spiral eyes flickered faintly, like coals burning low in a dying hearth.

"If you will accept my guidance—"

The shadows bobbed their heads in unison, a whisper of movement that stirred the snow at their feet.

"Do not give in to the temptations you might find inside."

Six pairs of shadowed eyes turned toward one another, and a pulse of cold radiated through the air as their thoughts aligned.

It shall be as you say.

For a heartbeat, nothing moved. The barrow loomed above them, heavy with age, its open mouth breathing a faint mist that smelled of dust, iron, and something older still, the scent of stone that had not known sunlight since the dawn of the world.

Meron drew a long breath and gathered his will about him like a mantle. It pressed close, invisible but tangible, a shield of discipline and belief. Even the suffron seemed to feel it, their eyes narrowing as the air thickened with the weight of his intent.

The magus placed his hand upon the latch. The metal was cold enough to bite, but he did not flinch. Beneath his touch, faint vibrations stirred, a hum like the deep exhalation of something ancient and aware.

He stepped forward.

The shadows stirred behind him, his soldiers shifting like ghosts. Then, with one last glance into the dim, trembling light of the snowbound world, Meron crossed the threshold.

The darkness beyond swallowed him whole, not a mere absence of light, but a substance unto itself, dense and whispering, alive with quiet expectation. It wrapped around him like a second skin, sealing the world behind with a soundless sigh.

CHAPTER TWO

Voices in the Silver Moon

The Silver Moon Inn smelled of roasted onions and damp stone, the kind of scent that clung to your clothes whether you stayed for an hour or a night. Outside, Ause City still lay under a sickly shroud of clouds, lightless and thick as wool, though it was well past noon.

Inside, it was warm. Safe, supposedly. But Rana wasn't fooled.

Rana sat at the end of the long bar, her boot tapping a silent rhythm against the floorboards. The common room buzzed with a palpable tension, low voices, and the occasional scrape of chair legs, but it all faded behind the pulse in her ears.

Her hands were clenched in her lap, fingers twitching with the ghost of power that wouldn't come when she'd needed it most.

Rhyslin stood nearby, nursing his second mug of water like it was something sacred. He hadn't spoken in a while. Just stood there, white hair tousled, posture carved from stone, eyes distant. She hated it when he went quiet like that. It meant something was eating him.

Her mother sat at a table with Flur and Rowena. Flur, golden and radiant even in tension, paced in measured steps. Ria, her mother, rubbed at her temples, the fatigue etched deep into her features. Rowena just stared at her untouched wine, lips moving in silent prayer.

They had all felt it, the ominous presence that had descended upon them.

But only Rana seemed to be seething with a fiery rage that threatened to consume her.

"That doesn't make sense," she snapped, glaring at Rhyslin. "It kept talking about suffering, how we'd suffer, how it wanted to make us suffer. Why?" Her voice cracked in frustration, too loud for the quiet room. She didn't care. "What kind of thing says that like it's a gift?"

There was a long pause.

Then Rembran's voice cut through the air like a blade through silk.

"Suffering lasts longer than fear," he said, not looking up from the table where his fingers traced an old scorch mark. "A wound heals in days. Fear fades in hours. But grief... grief can hold on for decades."

He looked older when he said it. Not in body, he was still built like the storm he'd flown through, but in the way his voice carried weight like he'd lived that pain.

"Parents and lovers," he added, "they suffer long after the body's buried. Some never stop."

Rana felt a chill skitter down her back. The fire crackled behind them, but it suddenly felt too far away.

"That's..." Rhyslin muttered, setting his mug down with deliberate care. "...diabolical. A being which feeds on something universal. If enough people suffer, it could grow endlessly. No limit."

His mouth curled in disgust. "What god would *make* such a thing? And why haven't we seen one before now?"

Rana didn't answer. None of them did. Her mind was back in the street, back in the moment when the shadows had swallowed everything, everything, and all she could see were the glamoured illusions of men, faceless and hunting her and the others like prey. Her blade had passed through the smoke. Her magic had faltered.

She felt herself shaking, small and contained but real. She clenched her jaw to stop it.

"I couldn't summon light," she said quietly, as if admitting weakness would call it back. "I tried. It just — wouldn't come. Like something was sitting on my chest."

Rhyslin turned to her then, eyes softer than she expected.

"It wasn't just you," he said. "I couldn't channel it either. Not properly." He paused, his brow furrowing. "Astinmah once said I was born of magic. But whatever that thing was — it felt oily. Greasy. The power slid away when I tried to reach for it. Like trying to grip a snake made of ink."

Rana blinked, swallowing. If even *he* couldn't channel, what chance had she ever stood?

She thought about the crystal orb. About how she'd shattered it midair, how the shards had cut into Sparhawk's cheek and drawn that moment of grudging respect. She clung to it now like a shield against the doubt trying to worm its way into her mind.

"I got one hit in today," she said. "Before everything fell apart."

He gave her a look, not pity, not condescension. Something else. Like pride tempered with worry.

"You got us time," he said simply. "Sometimes that's the only kind of victory we get."

The silence settled again, thick as the unnatural fog still blanketing the city.

Somewhere behind them, Flur muttered a curse under her breath.

Rowena reached for Ria's hand.

And Rana, for the first time, since stepping into the bar, let out a breath she didn't know she'd been holding, a testament to their resilience in the face of adversity.

The mead was warm, golden, and just sweet enough to dull the aftertaste of ash still lingering at the back of Marcus' throat. He took a slow sip, the weight of the wooden mug solid in his hand, the edge smooth from years of use. The hearth cracked behind him, casting flickers of orange against the tavern's stone walls. The Silver Moon Inn was quieter than usual, too quiet, even for a place full of survivors. But their determination was unwavering in the face of darkness.

He glanced at Rhyslin, who stood across from him, nursing water like it was a sacrament. Marcus understood why, even if he didn't agree. Rhyslin carried the weight of a thousand oaths; Marcus had learned long ago how to carry only what was his.

"Natolie was able to draw her blade and strike it," he offered, breaking the silence.

Before Rhyslin could reply, the familiar sound of soft boots on wood approached. Arms wrapped around Marcus from behind, her fingers weaving gently over his chest. The scent of pine and steel filled the space around him, familiar and grounding, hers.

"For all the good it did me," Natolie murmured into his shoulder. Her voice was low, rough at the edges. "Whatever that thing was, it took my strike and laughed at me."

She rested her head against him, and he leaned back slightly, giving her that space without making a show of it.

"You don't know how happy I was to see you guys," she added, just above a whisper.

Across the table, Flur gave a single, solemn nod. Ria exhaled softly, brushing her fingers against Rowena's, who still hadn't spoken since they entered. Even Rana, normally full of restless fire, sat unusually still.

It hadn't been the fear of shadows Natolie felt. He knew that. She was a hunter of shadow, born to silence, trained to strike from darkness. But what they'd faced, it twisted the dark into something vile. Something wrong. The fear she felt was that of someone who understood the shape of shadow and knew this wasn't it.

"You did good," Marcus said gently.

She snorted, but her cheeks flushed just a little, and she tightened her hold around him. Her blouse rustled softly with the movement.

"You held the line," he continued. "Kept the others close. Kept them alive. That counts."

Rhyslin nodded, his expression unreadable but sincere. "He's right. You struck it. I couldn't even touch it. Only one who landed a real blow was Andros."

He tilted his head toward the elemental who was sitting a few stools down, still dressed like a Wildman of the northern plains, furs dusted with dried flower petals, dark hair braided with copper bands. Andros beamed at the attention, practically glowing.

"Oh, stop, Maighstir Rhyslin," Andros said, waving a broad hand. "It was the least I could do. You've given Ixa and me so much already."

Rhyslin started to protest, Marcus knew that look, but Andros cut him off with a lifted palm.

"You gave us a chance to leave the place where time never moved," he said firmly. "You gave us purpose—a home. Let us roam the skies and feel change under our feet. That's more than we ever dreamed."

Rhyslin opened his mouth, but when Andros narrowed his eyes in that quiet, rooted way only an Earth Elemental could, the mage closed it again.

"Trust me," Andros added, his voice softening. "We couldn't be happier."

A hush settled over the table.

The fire popped, a single ember leaping toward the ceiling and dying in the air.

Marcus took another sip of mead, let the warmth settle in his chest, and looked around the circle at friends, survivors, and bonds both sacred and hard-won. The threat was still out there. The shadows hadn't vanished.

But for now, they had light, and each other.

Before he could say anything more, before he could argue the way he always did, Rhyslin felt a familiar tug deep within his chest.

A bond.

Warm, steady, unmistakably her.

He didn't hesitate. He let himself slip into it, into her, into the thread of golden light that was Ria, and her voice rose in his mind, firm but tender.

{He's right, mo chridhe[1]. You shouldn't argue with a man who's thanking you.}

---

[1] My heart

Rhyslin exhaled through his nose, a wry smile twitching at one corner of his mouth. She wasn't wrong. She rarely was.

{*You're right,*} he replied, letting the words echo across the tether between them. {*And thank you — for keeping me from making an arse of myself.*}

Her answer wasn't words at first; it was warmth. A gentle current of love and trust seeped through the bond and settled into his bones like a well-worn cloak. He felt his heartbeat slow, his shoulders ease.

{*I still don't get it,*} he sent, quieter now. {*Why did you give up your crown. You're a natural-born diplomat, Ria. You could have ruled for decades more.*}

He looked across the table, and there she was, Ria, seated with the others, her auburn hair falling in soft waves around her shoulders. She wasn't looking at him, not yet. But he caught the faintest blush rising on her cheekbones, blooming like the first hint of sunrise.

She never quite knew what to do with sincere praise. That vulnerability that honesty, it was something Rhyslin cherished more than he could say.

This time, she didn't hide behind formality or coy deflection. She turned her face toward him, and her eyes locked on his. Steady. Certain. Her smile was gentle and impossibly real.

{*You know why,*} she said. {*I always thought I'd die alone. I don't anymore.*}

A pause.

{*I love you, Rhyslin. Maighstir of my heart.*}

The words struck something deep inside him, deeper than any blade could reach. For a moment, everything else, noise, flickering firelight, even the dull ache of his own doubts, fell away. There was only her.

He held her gaze for a long, quiet moment. No need to speak. The bond said everything.

Finally, he turned back toward Andros, who was still basking in the praise like a cat in sunlight. The Elemental's clothing was wild and ceremonial, draped in plains-beast fur and heavy with copper bangles. There was no arrogance in his expression. Only quiet joy.

Rhyslin gave him a solemn nod, one man to another. One soul to another who had suffered and come through the storm changed.

Andros straightened in response, pride in his posture but reverence in his eyes. He wouldn't call it a victory; he respected Rhyslin too much for that, but the moment passed between them, nonetheless.

Acknowledged. Understood.

CHAPTER THREE

The Barrow of Trials

Meron stepped into darkness, trusting that the spider-god would watch over him. The air closed around him like damp cloth, heavy, still, and smelling faintly of dust and age. The darkness was so absolute that even the god's granted dark sight failed him; it pressed against his eyes like a weight, swallowing shape and distance alike.

With only the barest pause, he drew the fractured mirror from his pocket and held it out before him. The glass was cool and rough around the edges where it had broken, and his reflection, what little he could see, wavered like oil on water.

"Master of all, great changer, one who is dark and light, but neither. I ask for sight to penetrate the darkness."

For a moment, there was tomb-like silence. His breath echoed faintly off unseen stone. Then, with the whispering sound of a breeze through a web, the mirror stirred, its surface shimmered and then brightened, spilling a soft, silvery glow into the black.

It wasn't true brightness, but it was enough. The light revealed a narrow corridor carved from rough stone, walls glistening faintly as if damp with old condensation. The floor dipped slightly, uneven beneath his boots, and the air smelled of earth long undisturbed. The corridor stretched onward, a ribbon of dimness that vanished into deeper shadow.

Behind him came the sound of silk shifting, a dry, delicate rustle against bare flesh. His bonds followed close, their whispered prayers rising in soft unison.

Each voice trembled with reverence, their devotion answered as small charms and trinkets began to glow faintly, joining the mirror's light like scattered stars.

The thought that he could have used draoidheil to summon light never even brushed his mind. That power belonged to his enemy, the false source, the corruption of what was divine. He would rather stumble blindly than draw on such blasphemy.

He took a quiet breath, the air stale and cold in his lungs, and began to walk. His steps were soft against the stone, the sound of them quickly swallowed by the weight of silence. He didn't bother to check for traps. After all, why would the barrow-builder trap the first step of the journey?

Midway down the hallway, Meron halted. Something shifted, faint, but unmistakable. The air brushed against his cheek in a slow, uneven pulse, like the barrow itself was breathing.

He lifted his eyes and saw a column of deeper black cutting upward through the stone ceiling, a shaft of darkness rising beyond the barrow's bounds. A cold draft whispered through it, carrying the scent of soil and old iron. He realized this was how the air moved through the tomb, not stagnant, but alive, circulating through hidden passages like veins through flesh. There must have been hundreds of such vents burrowed into the outer husk. Whoever had built this place had designed it to endure. It was more than a resting place for the dead; it was a body, a mind.

With a thoughtful nod, Meron pressed onward, his soft footfalls swallowed by the hush. Behind him came the subtle rustle of silk and armor, his bonds first, then his thirty-one soldiers, and finally the five suffron, their presence felt more than heard. The sixth had touched the group mind for a heartbeat before returning to its hunt in Ause City, a thread briefly woven and then withdrawn.

The corridor ended in a wall of steel that shimmered dully in the mirror's pale light. Etched across its surface was a pattern of glyphs, each stroke fine as a spider's leg. Meron's eyes lingered over them, translating in slow, reverent silence as he traced their meanings with his mind:

Ever Changing
Never Ending
All encompassing.
Cocooned eternally
Woven through ages
Found by few

The Eight-legged One

Here with you.

This test, the first of four,

Take you nothing from the floor.

A slow smile crept across his lips as he read the last line again. "So be it."

Turning to his party, his voice carried the calm authority of ritual. "Touch nothing at all. Leave it where it lies."

His bonds bowed their heads, the silk at their throats whispering agreement. The soldiers straightened, silent and ready.

And within the half-light, the suffron shimmered faintly, those shadow-born children of Iktomi's flawed weaving, their collective thought forming a single response that brushed against his mind like a web-thread drawn taut:

We will touch nothing.

Steeling himself, Meron turned back to the door. He laid his fingertips upon its center. The metal was cold, thrumming faintly beneath his skin, as if some great mechanism slept within.

For a heartbeat, nothing moved. Then came a pulse, a deep, resonant throb like the echo of a drumbeat through stone, and the door began to stir. It crept open with a groan that reverberated down the corridor, releasing a draft of air that smelled of dust, silk, and secrets older than faith itself.

The darkness of the hallway broke suddenly into light so fierce it felt like a blow. Meron raised a hand against the glare, eyes narrowing as they adjusted.

A host of draoidheil orbs hung high above, their cold, steady light bouncing from flat mirrors set along the walls. The reflections ricocheted from surface to surface until the entire chamber shone like a forge of false daylight.

The brightness revealed mountains of treasure: gold coins spilling like water across the floor, silver ingots stacked like altar stones, sheets of copper glimmering in neat rows. Piles of gems, some uncut, others worked into filigreed jewelry, overflowed from low tables in the center of the room. The air itself seemed thick with metallic scent, sharp, dry, and tainted with the faint hum of draoidheil energy.

Meron ignored the glittering excess and walked forward, boots crunching against the occasional coin. Gold and silver had never stirred him, save for what they could buy in draoidheil components. Even now, the sight of such abundance felt hollow, an empty echo of divine creation.

He slowed as he neared the tables and half-turned to study his followers. Removing fear from them had not made them mindless; they were still capable of thought, of choice. Faith demanded that choice.

His gaze lingered first on his bonds, veiled figures moving with quiet grace. They lifted their skirts as they passed through the drifts of coins, stepping lightly over the gleaming mounds without hesitation. Their composure pleased him. *Faith refined through trial,* he thought, *is faith proven.*

The fair-haired bond did not so much as glance at the jewels. She walked past them as though they were dust and joined him at the far door. The dark-haired bond paused only long enough to cast a brief, dismissive look at the tables.

"You've given us better than this," she murmured as she came to stand beside him.

Meron said nothing, but the corner of his mouth twitched, not in pride, but in recognition.

The soldiers followed next, their boots clanging against the scattered treasure, coins skittering and ringing across the stone. They neither revered nor rejected wealth; it was simply in their way. Had the ingots been softer, they would have crushed those too beneath their heels.

And then came the suffron, formless silhouettes, the spider's imperfect progeny. They drifted through the chamber without pause or care. The gold was meaningless to them; its shimmer was no different from shadow.

When the last of them had joined him, the steel door ahead began to shimmer. Fine lines of light crawled across its surface, shaping into a verse written in spidery glyphs that pulsed once, like a heartbeat, before holding still:

Temporal wealth
You have declined,
This is a perfect
Frame of mind.
Of gold, silver, and jewels
Away you fell —
But can you resist
What the past does tell?

The words faded, leaving the metal smooth once more. The door slid open on silent hinges, and beyond it waited only darkness, deep, quiet, and absolute.

As if the rejection of the first temptation had lifted some veil, the darkness of the hallway gave way to a gentler light. Shimmering candles burned behind crystal lenses set into the walls, their flames steady and pale. The light spilled across the stone like liquid gold, wavering softly as Meron passed.

He slowed beside the first lens and brushed his fingertips across it. The crystal was smooth and cool beneath his skin, faintly humming with restrained warmth. The flame within danced steadily, untouched by draft or soot.

"How does the air reach it?" he murmured under his breath. "Who tends the wick?"

The questions lingered, half-spoken thoughts that pressed at the edges of his disciplined mind. No answer came. The air smelled faintly of wax and dust, yet there was no smoke. Everything was *too clean,* too precise, as though time itself refused to touch this place.

He drew a slow breath and pushed the thoughts aside, storing them in the quiet recess where all his troublesome curiosities went to war with themselves. Let the mind labor over mystery; the soul had work yet to do.

The corridor was short, the light ahead softening into a pale haze. When he reached the next door, he found it waiting, tall, smooth, seamless.

He raised his hand, but before his fingers met the metal, the door stirred of its own accord.

Without sound or visible mechanism, it parted for him, its movement smooth as breath. Beyond lay another darkness, quiet and waiting.

With a prayer on his lips, Meron stepped through the door, and stopped.

Before him stretched a chamber vast and quiet, its walls lined from floor to ceiling with books. Shelves climbed three levels high, vanishing into shadowed alcoves above, and dipped one level below into a sunken ring of more shelves half-hidden by darkness. The air was thick with the scent of beeswax, aged leather, and the faint sweetness of papyrus. It smelled of ink and dyes, of parchment long handled and well-loved, the perfume of memory itself.

Meron drew in that scent like breath, steadying himself. This was his paradise. His pulse slowed, his body relaxing without permission. Here, among these tomes, he could almost forget why he'd come.

Not only he, but his bonds also—those who had shared his long nights of reading and quiet study. He could sense their yearning as surely as his own. The air shimmered faintly, and he fancied he heard the faint susurrus of voices between the shelves: the books calling to him, whispering in a dozen tongues, promising to reveal what had been, what was, and what might yet come to pass.

He took one slow step forward. Then another. "Please, master, let me not fail. In your holiness do I trust."

His voice trembled just enough to betray him. As if feeling his weakness, his bonds began to murmur prayers of their own, low, earnest voices rising in unison. They prayed not only for themselves, but for him, their master who walked the edge of devotion and desire.

With each step he took, Meron could feel the faintest tug, threads of unseen force reaching out from the shelves, brushing against his mind. The knowledge within these volumes yearned to be known, to be touched. And he, in his heart, promised them silently: *One day. One day, I will read you all. But not today.*

Behind him, the steady cadence of soldiers' boots struck the stone—an anchor that steadied his thoughts, grounding him in the present. The suffron followed last, gliding like dark phantoms through the dim light. They gave no sign of recognition, no hunger for the wisdom that tempted others. Their indifference unsettled him. What, he wondered, could ever drive such creatures to frenzy? And did he truly wish to witness it?

At last, the path brought him to the far door. Its surface shimmered, and new lines of spidery script unfurled across the steel, burning softly as if written by invisible flame:

The call of the past
You refused to hear.
Well you've done,
My servant dear.
To this point,
None you've lost.
Can it continue,
Or will you pay the cost?

Ware the next test,

Some will fail.

The call for power

Will raise a wail.

Loss of fear is

An awesome thing,

But it can be dangerous

As a cursed ring.

When the final word faded, the door gave a sound like a sigh and parted down the center. The darkness beyond was absolute, silent, watchful, and waiting.

Meron squared his shoulders, drew a breath thick with ink and candle wax, and stepped forward once more.

The next corridor stretched scarcely twenty-five paces, yet each step carried the weight of ages. Along both walls hung battle standards from forgotten wars, silken banners faded to ghostly hues, the emblems of gods and kingdoms that had long since passed into dust.

Some bore the marks of noble lineages, others the sigils of chaos, but all were displayed with reverent care.

Among them, half-torn and brittle with time, hung a tattered flag woven with the eight-legged sigil of the spider-god. Its threads stirred faintly, as though remembering a wind that no longer blew.

As they neared the door at the corridor's end, the low, haunting sound of distant horns drifted through the air. It was not loud, merely the echo of a memory, but it sent a shiver down the spine of every soldier present. The door before them opened of its own accord, its hinges silent as breath.

With measured steps, Meron crossed the threshold. He expected smoke, the stench of battle, or the whisper of old ghosts. Instead, the chamber beyond stood pristine and still.

Ranks of terra-cotta soldiers filled the room, each sculpted with precision, faces stern, weapons poised, armor bearing the marks of countless forgotten cultures. In the center rose a raised dais upon which rested a man-shaped figure, its chest covered by an ornate breastplate of bone and darkened leather. The craftsmanship was exquisite: the armor of some ancient champion, preserved as offering or warning.

Meron's gaze lingered. He found himself wondering whether the warriors of old had once looked upon such relics with pride, or fear. To him, armor was a tool; to soldiers, it was lineage. And he, though commander, was no soldier by heart.

The faint rustle of lace brushed against the silence, reassuring him that his bonds followed.

The three of them passed among the statues without pause, their expressions serene, and took their place near the far door. There they turned, waiting. Meron, curious, wanted to see how his men, his living reflection of order, would respond.

The soldiers advanced slowly, their boot falls echoing off the stone. The removal of fear had not made them mindless; it had stripped away hesitation, not will. As they moved between the ancient effigies, the terra-cotta eyes seemed to wake. Clay cracked, light shimmered, and one by one, the statues reshaped themselves—helmets brightening to steel, shields gaining new polish, tunics bleeding into the crimson and sable of modern Saorsan garb.

When the soldiers reached the dais, they paused, every one of them raising a hand in the Saorsan salute to the relic upon it.

Meron's lips tightened in faint dismay. *He'd have to make a new salute,* he thought, one worthy of the spider-god's chosen, not the memory of a mortal empire.

As the last man lowered his arm, the ancient armor upon the dais began to change. Bone turned to burnished plate, leather to polished mail. A helm closed over the faceless head, and a great kite shield unfolded, gleaming with the spider-god's emblem.

Then, as one, Meron's soldiers turned and saluted *him.*

For a long moment, he said nothing. The weight of what he saw, the living and the dead united in a single gesture, struck him like the tolling of a divine bell.

Behind them, the suffron drifted in silence, untouched by pageantry or meaning. They moved as shadows, content in their alien indifference.

Meron allowed himself a small, satisfied smile and turned toward the far door. There, upon the steel, spidery lines of verse unfurled in pale light:

Thrice tested,
Thrice vetted,
Thrice loyalty
Has been tested.
Yet two more
Wherein you
Might be bested.
Can you survive
Through the dread
Of minions of mine
That haven't been fed?
If ancient hunger
You can best,
You will gain
After the final test.
My blessings will upon you be,
And you will take all you see.

The words pulsed once, then faded into the metal.

Beyond the door, the air seemed to stir, warm and fetid, like the breath of something vast waiting to be roused.

Meron inhaled once, steadying himself.

"Then let the fourth be done," he murmured, and stepped forward into the waiting dark.

46

CHAPTER FOUR

Song in the Dark

The windowpane was cold against Rana's fingertips, slick with the breath she hadn't realized she was holding. Frost filmed in a crescent where her hand rested, blurring the view beyond. Outside, Ause City remained cloaked in impenetrable dark, no stars, no moonlight, not even a flicker of distant lanterns. The black pressed at the glass like a living tide, a weight that seemed to push back with quiet insistence until the pane gave a faint tick in its frame. Smoke from the hearth drifted low through the room, sweetened with wood resin and the metallic tang of warming iron.

She sat at Rhyslin's side, drawn to his stillness even as unease twisted in her chest. When her voice came, it seemed to move through wool and ash.

"When will this darkness end?"

Beside her, Rhyslin didn't answer right away. His gaze held the void as if it might blink. The firelight painted copper into the lines at his temples; his expression had the set of carved stone.

"When the creature wants it to end, I guess," he said eventually, his voice like distant thunder, low and resigned. "Maybe when it's fed its fill."

Fed. The word curled in her stomach and went cold. The room seemed to tilt with it, the shadows lengthening just a fraction.

The front door groaned open, hinges complaining in a long, echoing sigh that let in a blade of night and a draft like a cellar's breath, soot, iron, wet rope. Candle flames bent toward the gap, and the fire muttered sparks.

Her hand drifted toward the hilt of her blade before the silhouette stamped a boot twice against the threshold and came through, backlit by wavering torchlight.

Lieutenant Sparhawk. Alive. Unharmed. The frost glittering on his pauldrons melted into threads that ran down leather like veins. He carried the same confident swagger he always did, as if monsters weren't hunting souls outside the threshold.

He scanned the room, a soldier's sweep, door, hearth, shadows, faces, until his eyes cut to Rhyslin. His posture snapped into ritual precision.

"Maighstir Darkblade," he said, offering a crisp salute. "Message from the council."

Rhyslin lifted two fingers in a casual reply, the gesture economical. The hearth popped.

"What is it, Sparhawk?"

The young officer strode forward, boots soft over rushes, and fished a folded note from his coat. Wax flaked from the seal like brittle petals.

"General Oberon wants you back in the council chamber."

Rana watched the small changes in Rhyslin, the flex of fingers, the slight deepening between his brows, as he skimmed the message. The light from the fire turned the parchment orange, pulsing with each rise of flame.

"Tell him we'll return when this darkness lifts," he said flatly. Then, with a raised brow that felt like a thin crack in granite, "Speaking of which, how did you get here without being devoured?"

Sparhawk shrugged with a crooked grin, breath fogging once in the draft from the door. A smear of soot creased his cheekbone.

"Torches. Iron blades. No draoidheacd. I brought a squad, trained, quiet, well-lit. Creature didn't bother us."

Rana's fingers tightened on the table's edge until the grain bit her skin. Pride and dread warred in the space behind her ribs.

"What is this thing?" Sparhawk asked, eyes narrowing. The torches he carried hissed softly, their resinous smoke threading the air.

Rhyslin sighed and rubbed at the back of his neck, thumb kneading at a knot that refused to yield. His breath steamed faintly in the drought.

"We don't know. Shadow-creature, we think. It feeds on suffering, plays on fear, illusions, glamours. Real enough to break someone."

That made Sparhawk pause; the grin faded to the memory of one. His jaw set, a line drawn with a knife.

"The council will want to hear that," he said, casting a measuring glance around the inn where faces turned toward fire or cup. "Everyone here safe?"

"Yes," Rhyslin said. "Everyone made it."

His gaze swept the room in a patient arc, Flur at the hearth, a small sun of calm; Ria and Rowena in quiet orbit over steaming cups; Natolie checked her blades with a clean metallic whisper; and when Rhyslin's eyes found Rana, she held his gaze. She didn't look away.

The near-silent clatter from behind the bar paused and resumed as if the inn itself listened and then remembered to breathe.

He turned back to Sparhawk, the fire drawing a soft glow across his knuckles.

"What can you tell me about the city?" he asked. "Any casualties?"

Sparhawk's shrug was less confident this time, his cloak shedding a line of melted frost that pattered like slow rain to the floorboards.

"A few. Stragglers mostly. People who didn't make it indoors in time."

"How many were women?" Rhyslin asked, voice quieter.

The question fell into the room with the weight of iron. Even the torches seemed to hush.

"I don't know," Sparhawk admitted. "The council didn't share that detail with me."

Rana saw Rhyslin's shoulders tighten, a minute ripple. A ghost of a frown drew and then faded.

"I'll tell them what you said," Sparhawk added, turning toward the door. "They won't like it."

Rhyslin snorted, an ember-bright sound.

"What can they do, throw me out into the dark?"

Before Sparhawk could reply, Rhyslin reached out and clapped him on the shoulder. The leather creaked under his palm.

"Be careful. That thing doesn't seem to care whose pain it feasts on."

The lieutenant grinned. A flash of teeth, quick as a match.

"There's little in this world that scares me."

He stepped forward and clapped Rhyslin's opposite shoulder, the two gestures ringing like a ritual exchange.

"But thanks for the concern, old man."

Rhyslin's eyes sparkled faintly, like fire glanced off obsidian.

"Old I may be, but I can still kick your arse."

Sparhawk chuckled, the sound easing the taut thread of the room by a hair.

"If you can't, you've got a backup." He jerked his chin toward Rana. "She can kick my arse for you."

Heat scrolled up her neck. She kept her chin firm, but her ears burned; the windowpane cooled under her palm.

"Be safe, spell blade," Sparhawk added, winking.

She nodded stiffly, swallowing the bright crackle of embarrassment with the smoky air.

"Let's move. One more message to deliver."

He called to his men; the torchlight tightened and drew away. The door swung shut behind him with a dull, decisive thunk, latching the night outside. The fire sighed. Shadows leaned back into their corners.

Rana exhaled slowly. The dark was still out there, pressing against the world. But so was she.

The silence that remained had weight. It settled on shoulders and into joints; the floor seemed to absorb it, old boards creaking softly as if they, too, felt the weather. Frustration prickled the skin between Rana's shoulder blades like cold sweat.

She crossed her arms, heel tapping a short, even rhythm against the wood.

"Why is that man so, so, frustrating?" she burst out, huffing through her nose.

Beside her, Rhyslin kept his gaze on the dying firelight. A smirk ghosted the corner of his mouth, here and gone like heat shimmer.

"He's from the far north plains," he said at last. "Beyond the mountains. Their kind are blunt. Direct."

His eyes flicked toward her with mild amusement. "And fascinated by strong women, it seems."

Rana tossed her hair over her shoulder, a sharp flick. Her cheeks warmed again despite the draft.

"Well, I'm not interested in him."

"Of course you aren't, sweetling," came a softer voice from behind.

A hand settled on her shoulder, warmth steady and immediate, the kind that sinks into muscle. Ria's touch always quieted the air around it. Rana leaned into it before she could stop herself.

Out of the corner of her eye, she caught Rhyslin glance at her mother; for a heartbeat she saw herself reframed, graceful, grounded, calm in a shifting room. The moment folded away like a page turned.

"Mother," she hissed, spinning toward her, "why would I want him when I'm destined to bond with Maighstir Rhyslin?"

Ria raised a brow, the expression amused rather than correcting and pulled her daughter into a loose hug that smelled of clean linen and rosemary.

"You don't know that" she said gently. "None of us do. Even Despoina sees only what she's allowed."

Rana leaned back against her mother's arms. Candlelight gilded the curve of Ria's cheek. Across the room, Rowena sat thumbing the edge of her cup, distant, as if listening to a line of thought run off into mist.

"I could ask Rowena," she muttered. "But she just says she can't see because of him." Her voice dipped with frustration. "That's not helpful either."

Ria chuckled, resting her chin briefly on Rana's hair.

"It's never easy, sweetling. The heart makes fools of prophets, sometimes."

The room inhaled and exhaled around them, the hearth cracked; glass clinked softly where Natolie poured tea; a rope of draft threaded the rafters.

"Momma — how many flings did you have before you met Garion?"

Ria pulled back just enough to look down, eyes bright.

"What makes you think I had flings?"

Rana gave her the deadpan only daughters manage.

"Come on. Flur told me about all hers. She said it's part of our nature. We test the wind before we set sail."

Ria's smile unfurled, warm as the fire.

"Three," she said softly. "I knew three men before I met Garion."

"Really?"

Her mother's arms tightened, gentle but sure.

"Nobody's stopping you from living your life, sweetling. The only one who's hesitating — is you."

Rana's nod felt like a small anchor dropped in a deep bay. She looked past her mother's shoulder to the man by the fire.

Rhyslin hadn't moved much. But she felt the gravity of him; even the lamplight seemed to lean his way.

"I want him, Momma," she said quietly, more truth than confession. "And only him."

Ria didn't argue. She kissed her daughter's hair and held her. Outside, the dark pressed its ear to the window and listened.

The fire's glow blurred against the Silver Moon Inn's polished wood, lacquering the tables with amber. Shadows swung lazily with each breath of flame; the room smelled of spice, smoke, and the sweet bottom of old mead casks.

Marcus sat at the far table with his chair tipped to watch the door without looking like he was watching the door. His mead had warmed to a dull sweetness he wasn't tasting. The weight between his shoulder blades, old campaigner's warning, hadn't shifted since Sparhawk left.

Footsteps approached with the rhythm he knew. He didn't need to look.

"Who's going with us?" he asked, voice low, eyes sliding to Rhyslin. The draoidh moved like a man bearing an invisible pack, heavy, old, and ill-fitted.

Rhyslin eased into the chair opposite, a careful lowering as if the wood might protest.

"You. Me. Rana. Natolie. Rembran. And Andros." A rub at his jaw, thoughtful. "The ones who tried to engage it."

Marcus snorted, dry as tinder.

"Engage it? I stood there swinging steel like a blind man in fog." He leaned back, gesturing with his mug, foam wobbling. "You, Rana, and Rembran tried the weave. Natolie actually hit the thing. I might as well have been comic relief."

Rhyslin's crooked smile was as tired as a camp at dawn.

"Don't be so hard on yourself, old friend. Your sword might've done more than you think." His eyes found the water in his cup and did not lift. "I couldn't even touch the weave."

Marcus studied the dull light lodged in his friend's gaze. Weariness, yes. But there was an edge of hollow, too, like a drum whose skin had loosened.

The floor responded to a new weight: a heavier tread, earth-solid. An herbal, rain-washed scent rode with it.

"I heard my name and figured I was being volunteered," Andros said as he joined them, folding himself into the chair like a boulder settling into riverbed.

"You heard right," Rhyslin muttered, raising a hand to the barkeep. The rattle of mugs on a tray answered. "Another round for the table."

Marcus drank. Andros watched Rhyslin with the same measuring look Marcus had given, only deeper, stone reading water.

"You look like a storm passed through you," the elemental said softly. "This thing outside... It makes me uneasy too."

Rhyslin nodded, fingers combing back his hair in a gesture older than the gray at his temples.

"Oberon wants us back at the council chamber," he said. "I suppose this," a small gesture toward the window where darkness pooled like oil, "Has him nervous."

"Smart man," Marcus muttered, setting his mug down harder than was polite. The sound was small thunder. "He should be."

The tavern maiden arrived, deft as a juggler, laying down fresh mugs that steamed and sweated.

Rhyslin nodded thanks; the water he chose might as well have been wine for how he held it.

"This isn't what I expected when we came here," he said after a while, voice nearly lost in the fire's whisper. "I thought we'd put out a fire and head home."

The words hung like unstruck bells.

A scrape of chairs: Rembran and Ixa slid in, the pilot giving a compact salute, Ixa shimmering like moonlight whittled to a figure. Ixa's hand came to rest on Rhyslin's arm, a touch like cool silk.

Rhyslin blinked, surfaced, and gave a tired smile that fit his face like a remembered habit.

Marcus leaned back and let his stare drift to the window. The dark offered nothing back. No movement. No flicker. Just a city-sized pupil dilated to the edge.

He didn't say it, but he agreed: they weren't going home soon. The room seemed to know it already.

The inn settled into the hush that comes when warriors stop pretending. The fire clicked and breathed; the stones returned warmth to the room as if reluctant to let it go.

Natolie stood at the bar for a beat, studying the way Rembran's shadow leaned toward Marcus, then cut across the floor to slide in beside the ranger. Her eyes kept skimming to Rhyslin as if he were a page her mind refused to turn.

"I saw Sparhawk," Rembran said quietly, voice tuned low to the room's quiet. "What's going on?"

Marcus sipped, wiped his mouth with a knuckle.

"General Oberon's recalled us to the council hall." He tipped his mug at Rembran, answering the silent question there. "You, me, Rhyslin, Andros, Natolie, and Rana. We'll go when, if, the darkness lifts."

Rhyslin didn't look up.

"If it does," he muttered, so soft the steam from his cup almost drowned it. His finger traced the rim, circling, circling. "We have no way of knowing when it'll end. Or what's keeping it here."

Natolie measured his shoulders: the slump under the cloak's edge, the way breath sat shallow in his chest.

"You're not acting like yourself," she said softly. "Rhys — what's wrong?"

He watched the surface of his water shift when he lifted the cup and set it down again. The motion looked like labor.

He's showing every minute of his age, she thought, not with years but with weight.

She glanced to Marcus. He gave one small nod, the kind they'd used a hundred times to say *yes, I see it too.*

"I'm just tired," Rhyslin whispered finally. "Trying to dispel that darkness around the creature — it drained me more than I expected."

Marcus raised a brow, old memory surfaced by a familiar bruise.

"Last time I saw you like this was at Tri Aibhnichean, when Astinmah tangled your access to the weave."

A ghost of a smile lifted one corner of Rhyslin's mouth.

"That was different. That was overuse." Two fingers pinched the bridge of his nose as if to squeeze pain into order. "This is — emptier. Like something took more than just magic."

Natolie felt cold start in her spine and walk outward to her fingers.

"Maybe when the darkness lifts," she offered gently, "it'll ease. The pressure. The drain. Maybe it's doing something to the weave itself."

"Here's hoping," Rhyslin said, forcing a smile that didn't quite catch, lifting his mug in a half-hearted salute. A yawn ambushed him; he hid it behind the rim, eyes watering.

Natolie held her tongue. There are no bandages for this. Only time. The tick of the wall clock suddenly felt loud.

In the corner of the common room, the lamplight softened to honey, laying thin gold on old knots and nicks. The Silver Moon's air wore the comforting blend of hearth smoke, spent candles, and a whisper of lavender from dried bundles hung near the stairs.

Ria sat with Flur, Rowena, and Rana, their chairs in a small citadel of wood and warmth.

Her ears were on conversation, but her eyes, drawn by a string she couldn't deny, kept slipping to him.

Rhyslin sat alone at a far table, half-turned from the fire. He cradled a mug of water like it might fracture. Shadows added years at the hollows of his cheeks; his posture ceded a little height with each breath.

"Flur," Ria whispered, leaning closer so her breath wouldn't travel. "Look at Rhyslin."

Flur's light banter with Rowena dimmed; her golden hair gleamed where the lamp caught it as she turned.

"He looks tired," she said softly, brow gathering. "Are we not letting him get enough rest?"

Ria parted her lips to answer, but Rana's voice cut in, tension like the plucked string of a bow.

"It's more than that." She leaned toward the fire's glow, eyes fixed on Rhyslin. "He's Mac Draoidheacd, right?" The nod around the table was a single ripple. "Could this be because he can't draw on ambient draoidheacd? If the weave's blocked by the darkness __"

Flur straightened, her eyes sliding from Rhyslin back to Rana with calculation and concern threaded tight.

"If that's true — then once the darkness clears, he should recover." A beat. "You've been pulling on the weave too, haven't you? How do you feel?"

"Other than being cut off? I feel fine." Rana's fingers tapped a soft, impatient rhythm on the table. "No pain. Just — like trying to cast into dead air."

Concern pooled between them, a quiet, pearly thing. Ria set her palm in the center of the table and closed her eyes. She reached, not with thought, but with that inward sense that felt like kneeling.

She sank into the bond.

There it was: the line to him, bright and strong, but carrying a borrowed weight that wasn't language. Not sorrow. Not fear. A tiredness that settled to the bone.

"No," Ria murmured aloud. "The bond is strong. But he's — tired. Deep down. It's in his soul, not his body."

She looked to Flur and Rowena. No words needed. Chairs whispered as they rose together.

The soft scrape made him glance up, slow as if returning from a long walk. He watched them approach, quiet behind his eyes.

Flur reached him first, her hand moonlight-light on his shoulder.

"Maighstir," she said gently, "we want you to come upstairs with us."

His gaze moved across their faces: Flur, Rowena, Ria, and for the first time in a long while, Ria saw all the small admissions the body makes when it stops holding the line alone: the tiny fold at the corner of the eye, the way fingers don't quite uncurl.

She stepped forward and offered her hand.

"Come, mo chridhe," she whispered. "Let us be your rest tonight."

A breath held. Then the release: he reached for Flur's hand.

"As you wish," he said, voice roughened by surrender and relief.

Rowena was already there, smooth as water, sliding his chair back and bracing his waist. The grace of it made help look like a dance.

Before they turned, Rowena's gaze sought Marcus where he sat still, sentinel to the hearth.

"When you're ready to leave," she said, calm as a sealed letter, "knock on our door. We'll make sure he's ready."

They led their draoidh into the stairwell's hush. Shadows received them like folded cloth.

Ria didn't know if the darkness outside would ever lift, but for tonight, they would do the lifting.

The fire had settled to a steady, low crackle, sending up a column of faint heat that made the air above it wobble. Shadows of chair legs and tankards stretched long and thin across the floorboards before giving up at the room's edges.

Rana watched Rhyslin disappear up the stairs bracketed by Flur, Rowena, and her mother. The three moved like the spokes of a wheel turning around him. They didn't look back. They didn't need to.

"Come along, my love," Marcus said next, his voice warm and frayed with a smile that had seen long nights.

Rana looked up just as Natolie flowed into his arms, her red hair catching the fire's light and throwing it back.

"Take me to bed, lover," she whispered against his cheek.

Marcus chuckled and scooped her up, looking like he had done it a thousand times. Their soft laughter floated up the stairs and vanished around the landing like sparks drawn up a flue.

And then there were four.

The inn's sound thinned. Even the clock's tick seemed careful. Ixa and Rembran leaned together, heads tipped in conversation that moved mostly through eyes and breath. Rana didn't listen. Her focus hovered on the space where the others had been, the ache naming itself only by absence.

She wasn't jealous. Not exactly.

Left behind, again.

She didn't blame them. Exhaustion required its rituals. Still, some part of her curled with the wish to be needed, to lay a hand where it would do good.

Time thickened. Rembran stood, she couldn't have said when, and offered a hand to Ixa, whose pale glow gathered itself.

"I think that's our cue," he said gently.

Ixa gave Rana a small, warm smile that landed like a blanket corner tucked under a chin. Then they were gone too.

Rana kept still. The fire whispered; a shelf creaked as the heat shifted the wood; somewhere behind the bar, a bottle clicked against its neighbor.

A low rustle.

Andros remained.

She blinked, surprised to find she'd forgotten the unmoving man, earth in a room of wind and flame. He sat folded and straight, a statue taught breath, eyes thoughtful but un-intruding.

"I didn't think you'd stay," she said, quiet apology in the words.

Andros tilted his head, a half-smile settling like a stone in a river.

"You looked like you needed someone to sit with you."

Her hands folded tighter in her lap, knuckles pale.

"I didn't want to be alone."

"You're not," he said simply.

The truth of it reached her, a warming stone in cold hands.

She rose after a long breath, the stairs waiting. Each step took and gave a small creak, the banister smooth under her palm from a thousand others seeking its certainty.

At the landing, hesitation pooled in her belly. *Go to your room.* The thought rang hollow. She didn't yet have one that felt like hers.

Candles threw soft ellipses of light along the corridor. Shadows slipped and re-formed with the draft from below.

A sound reached her then.

A song.

Soft, wordless, made of breath and something older than language. It drifted from the door at the hall's end, left ajar as if the room itself needed air. Their room. The one she shared when she was welcome and brave enough to claim it.

She moved on quiet soles. The melody unfurled wider as she neared, weaving warmth into the cool hall.

She peeked through the slender gap. Her heart thudded and then stood still to listen.

Flur sat with her back to the far wall, legs folded, Rhyslin's head cradled in her lap. Gold spilled over her shoulder; her fingers combed his hair with careful circles. He had let go of his guard. In sleep, he looked younger by entire winters.

The sight struck clean, envy and ache and reverence in a single breath.

Flur's voice filled the room like steam and starlight. Everything felt consecrated, the hush, the glow, the attentions of women in their own temple. Rana understood, with a pang, that she was peering into a sanctuary not meant to be broken by hesitation.

You're not one of them, not yet.

She eased back from the door and slid down the wall opposite, drawing her knees up and curling around them. The melody reached her anyway, a shawl of sound. She didn't cry. She held breath after breath until the song faded into simple quiet and her pulse stopped echoing in her ears.

Upstairs, the suite held the warmth like cupped hands. The lamplight drew soft halos on stone;

lavender drifted from a bundle hanging near the bed frame. The outside darkness pressed against shutters that gave not at all.

The door clicked shut; the room exhaled.

Ria turned at once and went to him, her arms sure, cheek to his chest, listening to the slow drum there as if confirming the beat kept. She exhaled, her shoulders easing a finger's width.

Flur slipped through to the bedroom without a word. He didn't need to ask what she gathered. He knew the rhythm of her care like a ritual.

She returned with a blanket folded just so, pillows stacked like offerings.

"Staying in new places is always interesting," Flur said with a teasing smile as she spread the blanket along the wall and ghosted a hand to smooth the corners. "But I'll always miss our big bed, my love." Her sapphire eyes sparked. "This one's too small for all of us."

The almost-smile that touched his mouth was real enough to count.

She settled with dancers' grace, legs tucked. Her palm patted the space where his head should be.

"Come here," she said, patting her lap. "Rest your weary head, maighstir mine."

He hesitated, the body counting costs out of habit. Then he sank to his knees, the floor cool and grounding, and eased down. Her fingers slid into his hair, firm circles at his temples.

The first pressure released the ache like a knot opening.

"I'll take it from you," she whispered, and then she sang.

The melody half-lived between breath and hum. It threaded along the cords of his neck and into the sternum where his breath had been shallow. Warmth rose under his skin, first in small sparks, then as a tide.

The ache lifted, buoyed rather than banished, carried as by gentle hands until it went weightless.

His breath stuttered and then ran then smoothed out. Sleep did not seize him. It welcomed him, arms open.

He sank deeper, the stone forgotten.

Even adrift, he felt the bond stir, silver strands tightening and pulsing in time with three familiar heartbeats.

Ria moved next, and he barely surfaced as she curled against his right side, her warmth humming low and steady.

Rowena's cool fingers brushed his temple. A kiss landed on his brow like a seal pressed into wax. She folded beneath his left arm with a precision that felt inevitable.

Flur's song dwindled; her hand did not leave his hair.

Wrapped in his women, the pain forgot his name.

Outside, the dark found no purchase to work its way inside the old, blessed stone.

Inside the suite, the air had settled into the kind of quiet that makes lamps burn steadier. Rhyslin lay with his head in Flur's lap, breaths deepening and lengthening into the rhythm of water over stone. Ria curled beneath his arm; Rowena fitted against his other side; fingers curled into his tunic as if keeping time.

Flur's fingers moved, patient and precise, ritual and love, each circle a promise kept.

A change of pressure at the door. She looked up.

There she was.

Rana stood just beyond the threshold, lamplight catching in her eyes. Her gaze walked the room, Ria, Rowena, Rhyslin, and something unguarded crossed her face and was gone.

Flur's smile was soft, a light turned outward.

"You can come in, Rana," she whispered.

The girl entered like a shadow taking shape, arms crossed, shoulders held in a posture that read as both armor and petition. Her eyes flicked to the blanket nest along the wall, then to the sleeping forms, and caught.

Flur said nothing more. She only gestured again, palm open over the prepared space, welcome made visible.

Rana's gaze snagged a second time on the space beside Rhyslin, then fell. She sighed, a breath small enough to hide in a fold of cloth and crossed to the far side of the room to change behind the curtain. Fabric whispered and stilled.

When she emerged, she moved to Rowena's side and knelt, curling with her back to Rhyslin, arms tucking around her knees like she could hold a fragile thing safe inside her ribs.

Flur watched for a count of heartbeats. Words rose and fell. Some things, even kindness, needed quiet to set.

Hang in there, sweet one, she thought, smoothing her palm once more over Rhyslin's brow. *You're already one of us. You just don't see it yet.*

She looked at him, then at the women curled around him, and finally at the girl a breath away. This is how a family is built—not with proclamations but with space kept, with small warmth's offered in the dark. Flur leaned back, heart aching and full, and she closed her eyes as the room breathed around them. Outside, the night pressed and was refused.

CHAPTER FIVE

The Betrayer's Gift

Meron stepped into the fourth chamber, expecting nothing short of an apocalypse.

What he saw was nothing, nothing at all.

No gold, no ancient texts, no soldiers, no light. Just a vast room full of absence, so complete it pressed against the edges of his mind. The air hung thick and unmoving, stale with the scent of stone dust and something older, like parchment left too long in the dark. His boots scraped softly against the floor, and even that small sound seemed devoured by the silence.

From the whispers behind him, he could tell that his bonds and his soldiers felt the same nothingness.

Their breaths came shallow, uncertain, as if the chamber itself were swallowing sound before it could be born. It was as if a void existed, some hollow that consumed both sight and sense.

When the shadow-beings shimmered past him, as if chasing something unseen, Meron blinked. Their movement left faint trails of dim phosphorescence, like moonlight dragging across glass. Why were they acting as if there was life down here?

The Suffron circled the room, wings flickering in slow, rhythmic pulses that sent shadows crawling up the bare walls. They moved with purpose, herding something into the center, something that did not exist.

But still, Meron had to ask.

"What are you doing?"

When the shadow-beings didn't answer, he closed his eyes and reached out with his senses. The world grew quiet.

His mind brushed the edges of reality like a spider testing her web for tremors. No, there was nothing there. No life, no pulse of spirit, no strands of the great web. Nothing had ever been in this chamber. The air itself felt untouched by time.

Yet the Suffron kept circling. Their movements grew sharper, more urgent.

"Enough of this," he muttered, lifting his hand. "Venerable spider who sees in the dark, grant me sight."

Power whispered through him, cold and fine as silk. Still, there was nothing, no flicker of the living, no echo of the dead. Yet the Suffron moved as if driven by instinct older than thought.

"Vharr—Skaeth!"

At his command, the shadow-beings halted mid-motion. The sound of their stillness was almost physical, like pressure easing in the ears. Slowly, they turned their faces toward him.

Why do you stop us from chasing our prey, Meron the Traitor?

Now that nothing was moving, Meron took a moment to examine the chamber. It was circular, seamless, the walls glistening faintly as though coated in glass. Faint patterns, spirals or sigils long erased, seemed to shift when he wasn't looking.

"What prey are you chasing?"

The Suffron shuffled closer to him, their knuckles brushing the cold stone. The spirals etched across their wings dimmed to a bruised blue.

We are hunting our prey. We sense fear but cannot feast upon it.

Meron glanced at his bonds with a raised brow. Both shook their heads, neither sensing life in this place.

"You have said that you cannot feel fear from us."

The shadow gave a slow, rippling nod.

That is correct. You are immune to our Pavor Umbrae.

"Have you been using your *Pavor Umbrae* since we entered the barrow?"

No, there was no need. Why use it when it doesn't work on you?

Meron looked around again, his gaze tracing the empty center of the chamber where the Suffron had been circling. The floor there seemed darker, as if light refused to touch it.

"Did you call upon it when entering this chamber?"

He was willing to bet the answer would be—

No, we have not.

"Then why are you chasing things that don't exist?"

The shadow-beings shimmered faintly, their forms rippling like heat over stone as they considered his words.

Because their fear called to us. It stirred our hunger.

Meron snapped his fingers, the sound sharp and startling in the hollow dark.

"You are being deceived. If there were things here, don't you think we would have reacted?"

The Suffron froze and closed their eyes. Their wings rose, curling inward like petals. The spiral designs along them brightened, then dimmed, pulsing in slow rhythm with their breath. For a moment, faint whispers, half speech, half sigh, stirred the dust along the walls.

Finally, they turned to Meron.

It is as you say. There is no food here.

Five pairs of shadowy orbs blinked, the light within them faltering.

Have we been found deficient in some way?

Meron shook his head slowly. The air stirred as if in response, carrying the scent of cold iron.

"No. You've been tricked, much like all people have been tricked."

He snapped his fingers again, a quiet punctuation that seemed to reclaim the chamber's silence.

"This is your test—to see if you can overcome your instincts to feed."

It is difficult. We sense the fear. It stirs our hunger.

Meron nodded. "Keep your eyes on me and follow us out of this part of the chamber."

He turned toward the far end of the room, where the wall dissolved into a black, seamless void. Even looking at it made his vision swim.

"What we seek is almost at hand."

Matching deed to word, he started across the empty chamber. The sound of his boots echoed softly, followed by his bonds, his soldiers, and the skittering forms of the Suffron. Their wings whispered against the air, faint as breath through silk.

If he was right, they would revert to form after passing the center of the chamber.

And if he was wrong… they might never leave this silence at all.

When the party crossed the line dividing the halves of the chamber, the world seemed to change.

The air trembled, soft and vast, as if some cosmic power exhaled into the emptiness they had left behind. A quiet pulse spread outward, invisible yet tangible, like a heartbeat deep beneath the earth.

The shadow-beings who had, moments ago, twitched and shifted now stilled, their restlessness dissolving into a reverent calm.

Meron closed his eyes, and for the first time since entering the barrow, he *felt*. The familiar hum of the celestial web returned to his senses, its threads brushing against his mind like silk drawn through fingers. It was fragile, almost shy, as if it feared to be noticed. He stood in stillness, savoring its return, the way a blind man might savor the first glimmer of dawn.

It was as if the rest of the barrow no longer existed, only this place, this air thick with memory and sanctity. The stale dust had given way to something finer, charged with the faint metallic scent of rain before a storm.

With reverence, the fallen magus stepped forward. His boots sank softly into the fine gray dust carpeting the floor as he approached the source of the hum, a colossal crystal case, half-buried in the gloom. It loomed from the center of the chamber like a frozen wave, facets glimmering faintly with internal light. Within it, suspended as though in amber, a splinter of power pulsed.

Each beat of that light echoed faintly through the room, casting ripples of illumination across the walls. Every surface seemed to breathe.

As Meron drew closer, the sensation deepened until he could almost feel a presence pressing against his mind—warm, immense, and sorrowful. He recognized it instantly.

His god.

His bonds stopped after crossing the boundary, the air too thick with power for them to continue. They held their positions, heads bowed slightly, waiting for his next thought.

The soldiers spread out around the crystal case, the faint scrape of armor echoing like a ritual chant. None spoke. The light caught on their weapons and helmets, outlining them in dim halos.

And the Suffron, those tattered, graceful shadows, stood before the crystal. Their wings unfurled in slow, trembling arcs, the spirals along them glowing pale blue. They tilted their heads upward, as if basking in sunlight unseen.

It is the master, but he does not answer.

Their voices filled the chamber like wind moving through hollow glass.

Why doesn't he answer?

The five shadows turned to Meron, eyes glimmering like dew on obsidian. Their hunger had quieted, replaced by something purer: longing.

Can you bring the master to us?

The question hung in the air, fragile as the web between stars.

Meron didn't answer at once. He stood before the crystal, the pulse of divine power vibrating through his bones. The god's presence, so near, yet so distant, was like standing beside the echo of a voice once known, now unreachable.

The silence deepened, layered and alive, as if the chamber itself awaited his reply.

Meron absently nodded as he brushed his fingers across the crystal case.

The surface was cool beneath his touch, smooth as frozen glass, but beneath that perfection something pulsed, faint, rhythmic, alive. He could almost hear the fragment within calling him, whispering in a voice made of silk and wind, telling him to—

The thought dissolved before it formed.

Following the call of the web, the fallen magus, turned disciple of chaos, reached into his pouch and withdrew the cracked mirror. Its surface caught the dim light of the chamber and fractured it into a dozen quivering shards that trembled against the crystal's glow. He knelt, reverently placing it before the case, and for a heartbeat the reflection of the chamber seemed to bend inward, as if the mirror hungered to drink it in.

Taking a step back, Meron bowed his head. The air pressed against his lungs, thick, metallic, electric. He drew a slow breath and traced a glyph through the dust at his feet, each line leaving behind a faint shimmer of residual power.

"Master, I humbly beseech thee to come to us. We — have a gift for thee."

The words rang out, swallowed by the chamber's immensity. His two bonds mirrored his movement, heads bowed, eyes closed, hands open in solemn offering. The soldiers, standing like carved effigies, raised their fists to their chests in ritual salute.

The Suffron remained closest to the crystal, wings outstretched. The soft pulse of their spirals glowed brighter, bathing the mirror in an eerie blue light. Dust hung in the air, as if time itself were holding its breath.

Then, the cracked mirror *shifted*.

Its angle changed without touch, turning ever so slightly toward the crystal, and from its fractured depths a faint image began to rise, like mist forming on glass. The air vibrated with a deep, distant hum.

{Where have you been, Meronkae? You disappeared from my web until mere moments ago.}

The image resolved into a shadowed figure, robed and cowled, its voice echoing through the chamber and through Meron's mind alike. The sound carried a strange harmony, as if a thousand whispers spoke each word.

Meron bowed deeper, voice steady but reverent.

"I have discovered an ancient barrow, my master. Within it, I have found what I believe to be a part of your divinity."

The cowled image leaned forward, the edges of its form rippling like smoke disturbed by wind.

{An ancient barrow, you say. Can you not bring the fragment to me?}

Meron shook his head, dust drifting from his hair.

"No, my master. The fragment is sealed inside a crystal box."

The chaos god smiled, a small motion that sent a ripple through the reflection, distorting his features into something half-human, half-spider.

{Do not touch the case, Meronkae. I will be there momentarily.}

Meron nodded once and stepped back from the crystal. The air around it hummed like a plucked string. The mirror's reflection deepened into blackness, drawing in the faint light of the room until only the crystal itself still glowed.

Then, as silence gathered, not the absence of sound but a dense, thrumming stillness, the cowled figure stepped forward, out of the mirror's frame. The glass rippled like water. Reality stretched, then *split*, releasing him into the world. Shadows clung to his form like oil.

A red-haired woman stumbled after him, pulled from the reflection by the hand that grasped hers. Her hair spilled over her shoulders like blood in water. Be silent, Priestess," the figure murmured. "I want you to witness this."

The woman covered her rounded belly with one trembling hand, her breath catching as her eyes darted over the chamber. She nodded, eyes downcast, to the cowled figure, who turned toward Meron.

"Meronkae," Iktomi crooned as he pulled the hood back, revealing a face of angular grace and cruelty. The spider tattoo between his eyes shimmered faintly, its ink seeming to move of its own accord. His gaze swept the chamber, lingering on the mirror, the crystal, the soldiers, and the Suffron. "You've done well, my disciple."

When his eyes fell upon Meron's bonds and the soldiers, his smile curved into something sharper. "You bring me followers." His voice was soft, delighted, and terrible. He leaned forward, examining them like specimens. "Oh, you've removed their fear. Very good, very good."

He completed his turn, his expression brightening as his gaze settled on the Suffron. "My children. My wonderful children."

The shadow-beings rippled toward him, bowing their dark forms in reverence. Their wings brushed the air, stirring faint drafts that smelled of cold stone and starlight. As they circled him, their whispers filled the air like the rustling of dry leaves.

The chaos trickster chuckled, a low, silken sound that trembled through the bones of the chamber. "You've exceeded my expectations, Meronkae." He glanced over his shoulder toward the woman. "How would you like to be my priest?" He gestured toward her. "It seems that Brigit wants not to be my priestess."

Meron offered a half-bow, head inclined. His voice was calm, his heart thrumming beneath his ribs like a distant drum.

"If that is your wish, my master. I will endeavor to fill the role."

The spider god chuckled again, the sound like silk tearing. He rested his hand upon the crystal, and the glow inside flared in response, flooding the chamber with golden light.

"Watch closely, Meronkae," Iktomi murmured, his voice low and fever bright. "You are about to witness something not seen since early in this world's history."

Meron said nothing. He could feel the web within him tremble as his god's power gathered.

Iktomi pressed his palm against the crystal. The surface rippled under his touch like water, and the fragment within rose toward him, vibrating in ecstasy.

He reached into the case, not breaking it, but *passing through,* and drew the splinter of power into his grasp. For a breath, it hovered in his palm like a trapped star. Then, with a smile both radiant and ruinous, he brought it to his chest and absorbed it.

Light erupted, searing and alive. The crystal darkened, veins of shadow spreading through it like cracks in ice. The air grew hot, metallic, reeking faintly of burning silk.

Before the witnesses gathered, the chaos god stood transformed, his aura vast and coiling, filling every crevice of the chamber. The light within him burned crimson and gold, the hue of blood seen through fire.

"I had forgotten this place existed, Meron." Iktomi drew a long, deliberate breath, and the entire chamber seemed to inhale with him.

The floor vibrated, the glyphs on the ground flaring and fading like dying embers. He lifted his chin, eyes bright with mischief and malice. "Now, Meron, why are my children gathered here instead of bringing chaos to the world?"

The air in the chamber had grown heavy since Iktomi's ascension. Threads of faint, silvery mist drifted down from the high vaults, curling and dissipating like cobwebs stirred by breath. The walls, once dead stone, now pulsed faintly as if veins ran through them. Every few heartbeats, a tremor passed beneath the floor, a slow pulse echoing the god's own rhythm.

Meron pulled his cloak tighter around his frame. The air was too still, the kind that muffled thought and breath alike.

His eyes flicked toward the Suffron as they lingered at the chamber's edge, wings half-furled, their spirals dim and expectant.

"If I may, my Master."

Iktomi turned his head. The spider-god's eyes caught the weak light and fractured it, scattering glimmers across the walls like sparks of ink. At his nod, Meron continued, his voice measured, calm.

"Death and Despair did them no favors when they dropped them in uninhabited areas."

He gestured toward the shadow-beings. They stirred at the motion, faint whispers of silk and shadow filling the air, like dry leaves moving underfoot.

"If you will permit me, I have an idea on where to send them."

The silence that followed was thick, almost tangible. Iktomi's eyes fixed on Meron, their glimmer narrowing to a single, piercing gleam. The magus stood tall under that gaze, though the weight of it pressed like stone upon his shoulders.

"If I had a map, I could show you."

At that, the spider-god's lips curved faintly. He lifted a long, black-nailed hand, and the air rippled. From the center of the chamber, shadows drew inward, spinning like threads into form. The shape solidified into an onyx table, broad and seamless, its surface glossy as still water. Symbols and lines etched themselves across it in glowing relief, rivers of light carving continents, coastlines, and names.

It resembled the ancient war-table from Long Sleep, but this one pulsed with modern life: a living map of the world as it now stood. The air above it shimmered faintly with whispers of the celestial web.

Meron stepped closer. The reflection of his face wavered across the table's surface, fractured by the glowing rivers that marked the Saorsa. His hand hovered over the map as though feeling the pulse of a living thing.

"There is one already hunting in Ause City," he said, voice low but tinged with quiet satisfaction. "I propose we send one to Hewes Town, one to Oak Grove, one to the Saint Ang Monastery, one into the old Empire, and one into the Ghalliad Confederation."

He spoke each name with deliberate precision. At every utterance, the map shimmered, and faint tendrils of shadow coiled over the marked cities, settling like stains.

The spider-god regarded the points of spreading darkness. A faint smile ghosted across his mouth, indulgent, knowing.

"So be it."

The words were soft, yet they carried through the chamber like the toll of a distant bell. The Suffron stirred, their wings unfurling in unison. The spirals along their limbs ignited with dim, pale fire, five silent flames ready to spread.

The air hummed with power as the black table darkened, its light retreating inward until only the five glowing marks remained.

Outside the circle of divine light, the rest of the chamber dimmed to shadow. The god's voice still hung in the air, and the faint webbing that lined the ceiling trembled in silent applause.

Meron bowed his head, hiding the faint curve of a smile. The first strands of Iktomi's dominion had been cast.

And somewhere beyond the tomb, across the hard-won lands of the Saorsa, five shadows began to move.

CHAPTER SIX

The Lifting of the Shadow

Rhyslin felt it the moment the magical darkness, a malevolent force that had shrouded the city, broke.

No sound announced it. No breeze stirred. But something primal within him recognized the shift, the moment the suffocating pressure that had shrouded the city dissolved, leaving in its place a silence so serene it rang in his bones.

He inhaled deeply, blinking away sleep as his senses re-calibrated. Across the room, Rana stirred at the same time, her breath catching softly.

They both felt it.

Rising without a word, Rhyslin turned first toward those still wrapped in sleep. Flur, his ciad-bhanna, had slumped against the wall sometime in the night, her golden head drooping gently to one side. Her hand still rested on his shoulder, a testament to their deep bond, even now, a bond that united them in this moment of peace.

He moved carefully, lifting her into his arms with a reverence few would ever see from him. The room was quiet save for the rustle of linen and the whisper of breath. He laid her gently between Ria and Rowena, adjusting the blanket over them all.

The three women curled in close, breath syncing in unconscious harmony.

A strand of Flur's hair had slipped across her cheek.

He brushed it aside, smiling softly as she murmured in response, a sound halfway between a sigh and a purr, felt more in the bond than heard aloud.

He leaned down and pressed a kiss to Ria's forehead. Her bond pulsed warmly in return, contentment wrapping him like a cloak. Then Rowena stirred, even in sleep, her own bond flaring with soft affection as his fingers traced the line of her lips.

He lingered for a moment, watching them.

He found himself pondering a question that had been lingering in the depths of his mind. When had his feelings for them transformed into something deeper, something he couldn't ignore?

Not in one moment. Not in some grand, explosive instant. It had been like sunrise, slow, inevitable, all-encompassing.

He turned, drawn by the faint rustle of cloth and a presence just out of rhythm.

Across the room, Rana sat in a patch of morning light, legs curled beneath her and a thick book open across her lap. She wasn't reading, not really. Her eyes moved, but they flicked up too often toward him, toward the bed.

When their gazes met, she blinked and quickly wiped at the corner of her eye. Then she offered him a wry smile as if daring him to mention it and dropped her eyes back to the page.

It pierced him in a place deeper than guilt.

Oh, mo phrìsei[2]. I know what you want. And if the time was right, if your heart were fully grown, I would give it to you in a heartbeat.

He crossed the room and sat beside her without a word.

She shifted almost imperceptibly and leaned into him, the top of her head brushing his shoulder. Her body didn't ask for comfort. It simply accepted his presence.

He glanced down at the book in her lap. The title, embossed in faded silver - *The Saorsa: From Wild Lands to Free Holds* by Oran na Saorsa.

A fitting choice.

"What do you think?" he asked quietly.

Rana looked up at him, her hazel eyes searching. "It's interesting," she said. "I didn't know your mercenaries bought the land from the Marquis of Bazan."

Rhyslin smiled faintly. "Marcus and I figured it was better to own the land than living in someone else's land."

Three soft knocks echoed from the door.

---

[2] My precious one

He stood, nodding to her. She nodded back and closed the book with care, marking her place with a ribbon before setting it on the nearby table.

The moment had passed.

But something had been seen. Shared.

And, in its quiet way, they accepted the moment, understanding its significance and the changes it brought.

Rhyslin stirred, reaching for his staff. His movements were fluid and efficient and unhurried, like a river returning to its natural course after being dammed.

She watched him for a moment.

From where she sat, Rana couldn't look away. He looked different now. Taller somehow. Sharper. Whole.

There was something in the air around him, a tension pulled tight, humming with power. The black smudges beneath his eyes had faded, and the flicker in his gaze, dimmed for days, was blazing again.

She slipped her own cloak from the table and fastened it around her shoulders. The wool felt warmer than before, the weight comforting. When she was ready, she turned to face him.

"Are you ready, Maighstir?" she asked.

"I am," he said, pulling the cowl over his head. The shadows beneath the fabric made him look older, more dangerous, like a story come to life. "The council will ask about your encounter with the shadow creature. Be honest. Say only what they ask. No more."

She nodded. "Yes, Maighstir."

Rana moved to the door and reached for the handle. Her heart beat a little faster, not from fear, but from the readiness to face the challenges ahead. She was prepared.

Or so she thought.

She opened the door and stopped cold.

Marcus stood before her, waiting patiently in the hallway. His silhouette was tall, familiar, every inch the seasoned ranger.

But for a heartbeat, no, two, she saw something else.

His face split.

Not violently, not grotesquely, but like light refracting on water, showing another truth just beneath the surface.

Half of his face remained the man she knew calm eyes, weathered skin, the slight crook in his nose from an old break.

But the other half was... lupine.

The wolf looked at her, not threatening, not snarling, but seeing her. In that moment, she felt exposed, her innermost self-laid bare.

Her breath caught, and she stepped back, blinking rapidly.

The vision vanished.

Only Marcus remained.

"What's wrong?" Rhyslin asked softly, suddenly behind her. His hand settled gently on her shoulder, grounding her.

Rana forced her breathing to steady, blinking once more.

"Nothing," she lied. "Maighstir Marcus just... surprised me."

She didn't look back at Rhyslin. She wasn't ready to answer the question forming in his eyes.

Marcus tilted his head slightly, watching them both. His smile was unreadable.

"When did you know?" he asked Rhyslin, his tone casual but his eyes sharp.

Rhyslin stepped forward, cloak brushing lightly against Rana's side. "The moment the darkness lifted," he said. "I could feel the weave again."

Marcus nodded. "You look better."

And it was true.

Even standing still, Rhyslin radiated strength. His shoulders were square, his breath calm and steady. The aura around him no longer flickered. It thrummed.

"I feel better," he replied.

Rana watched them both, her maighstir and the ranger whose soul bore another shape. The world was shifting. She could feel it in her bones.

Rhyslin looked toward the stairs. "Then let's not keep the council waiting."

And just like that, they were moving again, forward, toward duty, toward answers.

But Rana glanced back, one last time, into the quiet room they'd left behind.

The air still shimmered faintly where the vision had been.

And she knew what she'd seen wasn't a mistake.

It was a truth the darkness had merely peeled back.

The chamber smelled faintly of ink, old vellum, and burned oil from the lanterns hung along the stone walls.

The larger council hall beyond remained locked and quiet, too vast for real conversations.

This room, smaller, private, and lined with long maps and old chairs, was better suited for truths that weren't meant to echo.

Oberon leaned over a wide table etched with topographical lines of Saorsa's many regions, his knuckles pressed to the aged parchment as he traced the familiar lines of the northern marches. Ten dead. Six women. Four men. And no answers.

He didn't look up when the door opened. He felt them before he saw them. That strange weightless hush that always preceded Rhyslin, like the world briefly bracing itself.

"Ah, there you are," Oberon said as they entered.

Rhyslin led the way, as always, his cloak still creased with travel, but the set of his shoulders was different, upright, alert.

The man had looked like a ghost two days ago. Today, his fire had returned.

The others followed: Marcus, ever wary and grounded; Natolie, quiet shadow wrapped in crimson; the elemental, Andros, trying to look smaller than he was. And the girl, the spell blade, Rana. Sharp-eyed and silent. Still watching everything.

Instead of the grand council entrance, they'd come through the side corridor, slipping in like ghosts themselves. Fitting.

"Thank you for coming, my old friend," Oberon said, gesturing to the seats around the main table. He nodded at Rhyslin, examining him more closely. "You look good for a man who faced down a creature most of us can't name."

Rhyslin offered no humor in return, just a tired nod. "I wouldn't recommend trying to fight that thing."

Oberon arched a brow and motioned for him to continue. "Go on."

"I'm not sure where it came from or what it wanted, but it dampened ambient draoidheacd." Rhyslin took a seat, the soft clack of his staff against the floor echoing slightly.

Oberon frowned. "How bad?"

"When I pulled on the weave, it felt greasy… oily." Rhyslin flexed his fingers, remembering. "The power wouldn't hold."

Marcus exhaled, his voice gruff. "Same for me. It was like trying to catch water with bare hands. Only Nat could land a hit, and even then, the damn thing laughed at her."

Oberon turned toward the red-haired Sealgair Aisling. "Shadow magic, right?"

"Yes, sir," Natolie said. "I struck it center mass. It didn't flinch."

He rubbed at his temples. He'd seen what her blades could do, watched them tear through a group of bone-stitched revenants like parchment. For something to shrug that off…

His gaze shifted to the youngest at the table.

"And what does the young woman who humbled Sparhawk have to say?" he asked, injecting just enough warmth to soften the teasing.

The girl blinked, visibly unsure if she was being mocked. But she recovered well.

Twisting a strand of hair absently around one finger, she replied, "I stayed back. Watched our rear.

Natolie was in front. She asked me to try summoning light, but…"

She looked down, voice quieter now. "Nothing came."

Her admission hung in the air, heavy with something unspoken. Shame? Guilt? Perhaps both.

Rhyslin studied her with quiet approval. Oberon noted it.

When the girl fell silent, the draoidh cleared his throat. "Oddly enough, the only one who could actually stop it was Andros."

Oberon raised his brows and turned to the elemental, who looked like he would have preferred sinking into the stone floor.

"How did you manage that when Maighstir Darkblade couldn't?"

"I… buried it." Andros shifted in his seat, eyes flicking toward the table instead of the general. "Formed a dome of earth around it. Made it mad enough to chase me."

"Through the planes?" Oberon asked, stunned.

Andros gave a crooked smile. "Lost it on Lasair. Fire and light there, it might've been too much for it."

Oberon stared for a beat longer, then nodded slowly. "Whatever the case, your quick thinking gave the others time. Not everyone was as lucky."

Rhyslin's eyes narrowed. "How many?"

Oberon didn't sugarcoat it. "Ten. Six women. Four men. The men died trying to shield them. The women… we think they died of fright. Wide eyes. No marks."

Silence thickened. Grief turned the air brittle.

"That makes sense," Rhyslin said grimly. "Ria and Flur said they heard the sound of wild men approaching."

"It was more than that," Rana said suddenly.

Oberon turned his eyes back to her.

"I heard them," she said, her voice thin but strong. "Footsteps. Shouting. Laughter. I could smell them, sweat and mead. I thought…" Her hands tightened in her lap. "I thought I was being hunted."

The whole table went still.

Oberon didn't speak. He let her words sit. This wasn't the kind of fear that vanished with daylight.

Rhyslin placed a hand gently on her shoulder, and she leaned into him like a branch bending toward the sun.

"So it feeds on fear?" Oberon asked.

"No," Rhyslin said. "Worse. It feeds on suffering. It spoke of it like — like a meal."

Oberon muttered a curse under his breath. "Any idea where it came from?"

"I haven't the faintest," Rhyslin said, shaking his head. "And I've no clue how to kill it."

"What about the gods?"

"They have their own battles."

Oberon didn't ask what. He didn't want to know. If the gods were busy, mortals were in trouble.

"So, what now?" he asked, folding his arms.

Rhyslin actually chuckled, the sound bitter. "We fall back on the old ways. Iron. Silver. Light. Shadows hate purity."

"Iron," Oberon repeated thoughtfully. "We use steel now. Better for forging."

"Yes, but the old Houses still hoard iron. From the corpse war."

Rana perked up. "What corpse war?"

Oberon blinked at her. "You're serious?"

"She's eighteen," Rhyslin said with a smirk. "She hasn't reached that part of her history studies yet."

Oberon sighed and rubbed his temples. "Gods save me. I'm getting old."

"She's learning," Rhyslin said. "One shadow at a time."

Rana's voice broke through the hum of quiet speculation, sharp with realization.

"Corpse war?" she asked, her tone rising. "Is that what Marcus meant when he said he thought you got them all?"

Rhyslin turned to her, a flicker of pride sparking beneath his ribcage. She was putting it together. Gods, she was quick.

"Very good," he said, nodding once. "Yes. The Great War, what most call the corpse war, was the same conflict. Saorsa was still young then. Barely twenty years old. And the dead — they came for us in numbers that made winter storms look kind."

He swept his hand around the room, gesturing to the ones who had lived through it. "Marcus. Natolie. Myself. We were part of the hunt. We tracked and destroyed the Skelletdrachen, the dracoliches who led the dead armies."

His gaze shifted to Oberon.

"Your grandfather led the campaign against the rest of the unliving."

Oberon's weathered face tightened with the memory, but he nodded. "He died taking down a Skellet-Zauber, one of the necromancers who raised the army. They don't leave wounds that heal."

Rana's hand fell instinctively to the hilt of her sword. Her fingers curled around the silver runes etched along the cross guard, and he could see the questions dancing in her hazel eyes even before she asked.

"Why was iron better than steel?" she asked quietly.

Rhyslin leaned forward, resting his elbows on his knees, his voice lowering into something close to reverence.

"Cold iron doesn't just pierce flesh; it unravels the magic that binds spirit to body. Draoidheacd blasé, we called it. The residue of soul-anchoring spells. Steel's harder, yes, but it doesn't hold runes long. Iron… iron remembers."

He paused, letting the weight of the words settle. Across the table, Oberon looked thoughtful, and even Marcus had stilled, eyes distant.

Rana blinked slowly, and her gaze met his. "You have iron weapons in the armory, don't you?"

"I do," he said softly. "A few. Swords, daggers, maces, relics from the war. Most were melted down or lost to rust. I kept mine. My staff," he reached out and brushed two fingers along the dark wood and iron latticework just below the rune cluster, "has a threaded iron core. That's why it holds so much power."

Oberon leaned forward slightly, eyes on the staff. "Do you think iron will work against this shadow beast?"

Rhyslin closed his eyes, picturing the creature again, the stench of it, the oily resistance in the weave, Natolie's blade striking true and being swallowed into nothing.

"It absorbed shadow magic," he murmured. "Steel didn't even scratch it." He opened his eyes, steeling his voice. "Yes. I believe iron will hurt it. But we'll need to find it again and test the theory."

Oberon ran a hand across his brow, fatigue showing in the lines around his eyes. "Very well. Please keep the council apprised of your progress."

There was doubt in his voice. Rhyslin didn't blame him.

"How long are you staying in town?" the general asked.

Rhyslin hesitated, turning slightly toward Rana. She was watching him; head tilted to the side like she was weighing something he hadn't yet said. He raised a brow in silent question. She only shrugged, but her posture, her hopeful restraint, said everything.

He knew that if they were bonded, he would feel her answer before she gave it, just as he knew she'd be thrilled to stay.

"I hadn't planned on staying long," he said aloud. "Maybe a week. I still need to inspect the new transport ship and cutters." He looked back at Oberon. "But if you need us, we're at the Silver Moon."

Oberon's eyes flicked briefly between him and Rana but gave no indication of what he saw. "Thank you, old friend," he said instead, tone formal but warm.

Rhyslin rose and gave him a nod. Duty done for now.

But he couldn't shake the weight of Rana's words earlier. That fear she had spoken with. The sound of boots, the scent of mead and sweat. She had felt the nightmare hunting her.

Rhyslin offered Oberon a warm nod, the edge of a wry smile tugging at his lips. "Think nothing of it, Cian."

The general murmured his thanks, already distracted with council matters, fingers drumming absently on the edge of the map table.

Rhyslin turned from him and tapped Rana lightly on the shoulder. She straightened at once, hazel eyes flicking to his face. The way she responded, attentive and bright-eyed, never failed to remind him how much she wanted to be at his side.

"Come along, Rana," he said, a thread of amusement in his voice. "Let's take a walk." She beamed, her cloak swishing lightly around her legs as she stepped toward the door. But halfway there, she paused, brow furrowing at the sound of quiet chuckling behind her.

Rhyslin had turned and now stood with arms crossed, watching Marcus, Natolie, and Andros give him the most absurdly expectant looks he'd ever seen. Marcus raised both brows. Natolie clasped her hands dramatically. Andros actually pouted.

He sighed, long-suffering. "Yes," he drawled, voice dry as the desert wind, "you can walk with us."

Rana laughed softly as they all scrambled to follow. Rhyslin shook his head as he opened the door, muttering under his breath, "Gods preserve me… adults acting like children."

Behind them, boot heels clattered across the stone, laughter echoing faintly as the door swung shut on the war room's dim lighting.

CHAPTER SEVEN

The Web of the Spider-God

Iktomi spread his fingers over the map of Saorsa and studied Meron's marked cities. Only one mark made him frown: the Saint Ang Monastery.

"Meron, why the monastery?" he asked.

The fallen magus opened his mouth to answer, then froze when the Chaos-god lifted a single finger and spoke to the woman at his side. "Brigit, fetch Saldren and Yarsmith. Bring them here."

Brigit pressed her hand to her belly and dipped her head. "Yes, Master." She stepped through the slit of portal the god had shaped and vanished.

When the ripple died, Iktomi gestured for Meron to continue. "The monastery houses two thousand veterans," Meron said. "They are tended by sagartean, chirurgeons, mind-healers, and hearth-maidens."

The god's eyes narrowed at the word *sagartean*. "A strike there will wound the nan-diathan and their followers," Meron added.

Iktomi tapped on the onyx table, listening to the soft, hollow echo as he weighed the plan. He looked up at the Shadow-beings gathered around the map— no faces, only intent—and found the answer in their collected hunger. "I concur," he said. Then, voice like velvet and iron, "You heard Meron, my children. Go. Cause chaos. Feed to your hearts' content."

The shadows crawled across the face of Crann Na Beatha, each moving in answer to the god who had shaped them, spreading chaos where they passed.

One slipped through the open gate of the ancient monastery on the hill. Like a snake it wound up the path toward the courtyard's door, gliding past sleeping trees and shrubs until it reached the old soldier dozing before the fire.

The flames bent low as it rose behind him, silent as death. Wings of darkness unfurled, their spiral orbs pulsing faintly before closing around the man's body. Then, without sound or struggle, the shadow sank into him, and the fire flared bright again, as if nothing had ever moved.

When the old soldier rose to his feet and stumbled toward the entrance, the shadow-being used that moment to settle into its new flesh. The man's body trembled, joints creaking like hinges long forgotten, as the Suffron learned the weight of bone and the rhythm of breath.

Once inside, it paused, letting the chill of the monastery seep into its stolen skin. The corridors smelled of wax and damp stone. From distant halls came the soft chant of evening prayers, the slow drip of melting tallow, the faint shuffle of sandals over worn flagstones. The Suffron moved in silence through it all, a darkness that absorbed the light around it.

It explored patiently. It found where the weapons were kept, racks of spears dulled by dust, and where the weak-willed were housed, their dreams thick with fear and failure. It lingered where the easiest swayed slept, tasting their slumber like a scent on the air. Then, with unhurried delight, it began to feed.

Using the soldier's memories, it sought the woman he desired. It followed her by the sound of her breath, the tremor of her candlelight along the walls. When it found her, it dragged her into a storage room thick with incense and old wine. There, in the dark, it whispered through the soldier's mouth until her terror grew sharp enough to flavor the air. She died of fright before it even touched her.

Inside, the old soldier watched every heartbeat of her dying, trapped behind his own eyes. When her body fell still, the Suffron drank deep of his guilt, its flavor rich and hot, before driving his own blade into his throat. His death was a soft, wet sound that echoed through the stone hall like a sigh.

It did not rest. For the next eight hours, it wore new bodies: an old soldier, a chirugeon, a battle-medic, a Sagart.

Through each, it hunted the hearth-maidens, using memory and longing as guides. The monastery was filled with muffled screams and the thud of running feet. Lamps were overturned, incense burners spilled, prayers forgotten. Fear thickened the air until even the holy water turned sour.

When the last woman's fear was consumed, the Suffron began to stalk the solitary, the men who had hidden themselves in prayer cells and alcoves. It fed on their whispered psalms, savoring the moment they realized the words no longer protected them.

By the time the sun began to sink behind the monastery walls, the survivors had gathered in trembling bands. The air stank of smoke and sweat, and the echo of weeping filled the courtyards. The Suffron sank back into the shadows.

It silently watched as the hunters turned on each other, suspicion spreading like fire through dry grass. Blades flashed in the half-light; blood darkened the stone.

When the last cry faded, it drifted among the fallen, feeding on the slow, rich pulse of their suffering.

Outside, the monastery bells tolled vespers, hollow, directionless, and not a soul was left to answer.

"I have returned, Master." Brigit intoned, one hand on her belly as she led Saldren – the half-drake, and Yarsmith – the Assassin, through the slit portal.

A rush of air followed them, cold, stale, and damp. The Barrow's breath. The corridor beyond was narrow, walls slick with condensation and carved through black basalt veined in dull red light. Each rune pulsed faintly, like a dying heart, the glow reflecting in small puddles that trembled at the sound of their steps.

The air smelled of burnt tallow, old blood, and stones that had never seen the sun.

From somewhere deep below came the slow, rhythmic drip of water, a heartbeat that belonged to the earth itself.

"Iktomi, if you've created more chaos, I'll —" Saldren threatened as he took a step into the darkness of the Barrow and paused. His nostrils flared as the stale air bit at the back of his throat. His voice echoed back to him in whispers, distorted, like the mocking laughter of unseen things caught in the stone.

At his side, the assassin Yarsmith merely shook his head and took a half-step to one side. His boots moved silently over grit and bone-dust.

He kept one hand near the hilt of his blade, though the gesture seemed more for poise than protection. The air here was heavy, the kind that pressed against the skin and made every heartbeat feel too loud.

Iktomi's eyes flashed red as he looked up from the map spread across the stone altar. The parchment lay pinned beneath cold iron weights shaped like spiders. One long finger hovered above the outline of the monastery. The air changed, not with wind, but with weight, as though the Barrow itself held its breath.

Frost blossomed along the edges of the map, delicate as spun glass. The smirk that crept across Iktomi's lips caught the light, and when he turned, the faint rasp of silk accompanied the motion. Shadows rippled behind him like living threads. His gaze settled on the half-drake.

"You'll do what, Saldren? Attack me again?" The spider tattoo across his throat shimmered, its ink moving as though alive. "That didn't work the last time, half-drake."

A tremor ran through the chamber, not an earthquake, but the subtle vibration of power held tightly in check. Dust drifted down from the ceiling in slow spirals. Along the sides of the hall, the soldiers who had come with Meron fixed their eyes on Saldren. Their armor creaked softly as they shifted, tension rippling through the ranks like a drawn bowstring.

Their breath fogged in the freezing air. One man swallowed audibly, the sound swallowed by silence. They waited for violence, or permission.

Meron's two bonds, lithe as spiders themselves, moved with perfect synchrony to clear the line between the soldiers and the half-drake. Their steps were soundless, precise, as though they could feel each vibration in the floor.

Delicate fingers dipped into pouches, palming spell components and small vials of quicksilver and healing salves, not for the Spider-god, but for their mortal master.

Meron himself looked up from the map, his expression unreadable in the half-light. The web-like tattoos on his fingers glowed faintly as he began to trace runes in the air. Each stroke left a crimson trail that hung for a heartbeat before fading with a hiss, like cooling metal. All it would take was but a single word from Iktomi, and all ifrinn would break loose.

Brigit, the witch-turned-reluctant-priestess, stepped forward. The hem of her robes brushed against the wet floor, gathering streaks of soot and dust. She raised her hand from her swollen belly and, with visible hesitation, touched Saldren on the shoulder.

Her skin looked almost translucent in the flickering light, veins faintly visible beneath. Her fingers trembled as if sensing the storm beneath his scales.

"Saldren, please, not here. He's too strong."

The words drifted into the chill air and lingered like smoke. The echo of dripping water filled the silence that followed, each drop punctuating the tension. The shadows along the walls seemed to deepen, the torchlight dimming until faces blurred, and only eyes gleamed red or gold.

The Barrow itself seemed to wait, a living observer, eager to see whether blood or restraint would define the next moment.

At her touch, the half-drake whipped his head to one side, the U-shaped horns threatening to sweep the priestess off her feet. "Be silent, woman. This is between Iktomi and me."

The spider-god's eyes narrowed slightly at the threat to his reluctant priestess. With a casual gesture, he summoned her to his side; the air rippled and she moved without walking, her body gliding as if drawn by unseen threads. He rested a possessive hand on her hip. "Be careful, Saldren." He hissed, voice soft but carrying the weight of command. "I have not given you permission to hurt that which is mine."

When Brigit cringed, Iktomi's gaze dropped, his head angling slightly as though studying prey. "What is it, my dear?"

"It is nothing, master," Brigit whispered, bowing her head. Strands of red hair fell over her shoulders, catching the faint red glow of the runes like fire behind smoke.

Dismissing the priestess with a flick of his fingers, Iktomi turned his attention back to the half-drake. "This my house, Saldren. I suggest you calm yourself."

Saldren drew in a deep breath, the sound rough in the still air, then exhaled through his teeth, a soft gust of heat that melted the nearest frost. "Why am I here and what have you done?" His voice, while not calmer, was cooler, a forced truce layered over molten anger.

"I am doing what you wanted," Iktomi said, glancing back down at the map. The frost retreated from where his hand hovered. "I am starting my campaign to retake my rightful place among Nan Diathan." He gestured to the map. "Come, let me show you."

The red light pulsed, steady and slow. Beneath their feet, the Barrow hummed, the sound low and endless, like a web vibrating under the weight of something vast and unseen.

Dust rose around Saldren's feet as he made his way to the onyx table and stood across from Iktomi. Each step echoed dully against the chamber walls, the sound swallowed by the heavy air. The Barrow still reeked faintly of incense and iron, the scent of old sacrifices and burnt offerings clinging to the stone.

The same dust was barely disturbed as Yarsmith followed the half-drake. His passage was quiet, almost spectral. He paused at the table's edge, the dim red light from the runes glinting off the edge of his dagger sheath and inclined his head in the fallen-magus' direction.

"Meron."

Meron returned the nod with a grunted, "Yarsmith." His eyes never left the map.

The map was spread wide across the table, its parchment shimmering faintly with threads of silver ink. Cities and borders pulsed like veins, the glow shifting in rhythm with the low hum of magic that filled the chamber. The onyx table reflected it all, a dark mirror where their faces appeared warped and doubled by the shifting light.

The assassin circled the table, each step soft but deliberate, to stand at Meron's side. The faint scent of oil and steel followed him, sharp in the cold air.

"All the major cities? But, why not Eola?"

Meron shrugged, shoulders moving beneath his ink-stained robes. "Not enough people to make an impact. Besides, the last time I heard, that was your territory."

Yarsmith bristled. His jaw tightened, the movement small but telling. A long moment passed before he spoke again, his voice edged like a blade.

"Circumstances compelled me to leave."

The magus nodded, a soundless gesture of acknowledgment. The dim light caught the rings on his fingers, each carved with a sigil, each faintly pulsing as if aware of the conversation.

"Master Iktomi has so informed me."

A silence followed, heavy as the stone above them. The faint hum of the runes deepened, as though the Barrow itself listened.

The map shimmered faintly, one of the silver lines, the one leading to Eola, fading until it disappeared.

Dust drifted again in the stale air, catching the red glow like blood suspended in water.

Saldren and Iktomi faced off across the onyx map table. The surface was dark and polished, its glassy sheen broken only by lines of dimly pulsing runes that crawled like veins across its surface. Faint light from the glyphs painted the half-drake's scaled jaw and the Spider-god's pale hands in alternating hues of red and black.

Dust drifted in slow spirals between them, disturbed by Saldren's measured breathing.

The chamber was silent save for the low hum of magic, a resonant vibration that seemed to come from deep within the table itself. It was the sound of something alive and aware, waiting to be obeyed.

The half-drake leaned over, examining the map. His eyes, molten gold in the half-light, scanned the four Saorsan points that glimmered faintly like embers trapped beneath glass.

The smell of cold iron and damp stone clung to the air. His keen gaze narrowed as he caught what others had missed, two additional points, faint but undeniable, pulsing beyond the Saorsa's border. One nestled in the mountains. The other flickered like a wound in the lands once ruled by the old Empire.

"You've sent something into the mountains and the old Empire." He glanced up at the spider-god, the reflected rune light shifting across the planes of his face. "What was it?"

Iktomi chuckled. The sound was quiet, but it filled the Barrow, smooth, deliberate, and faintly inhuman. "Astute, as always, Saldren." His praise was sheathed in a cool tone, more mockery than approval.

His eyes gleamed red in the onyx reflection, twin sparks beneath the hooded calm of his expression.

"My pets have infiltrated two of the target locations and are causing chaos." He extended one long, pale finger toward the map, the movement graceful and precise. The runes flared faintly at his touch, responding like living threads of his web.

He pointed toward the old monastery. "In fact, one of my pets has fed very well there."

The air grew colder, heavy with a faint tang of ozone. Frost ghosted along the map's edges, tracing the outline of the Saorsa and its neighboring lands. The light dimmed to a pulse, and in the momentary darkness, it was hard to tell whether the faint chittering sound that followed came from beneath the table, or from the Spider-god's throat.

CHAPTER EIGHT

The Taste of Happiness

Rana hadn't expected to follow him.

After the council meeting, she'd stayed quiet, watching Rhyslin linger near the square as the others veered toward the inn. She could feel it, the way he let the crowd swallow him, not out of discomfort but curiosity. He always did that when something was pulling at his thoughts.

So, she followed.

The streets of Ause City were alive with late-day hustle. Lanterns flickered to life in the windows overhead as vendors called out final bargains, trying to sell off produce and bread before nightfall. The scent of grilled meats, roasted chestnuts, and sun-warmed fruit mingled with the cool breath of evening. Children darted past, laughing, while shopkeepers pulled canvas tarps halfway down over their wares.

Rhyslin moved like water through it all, measured, calm, unhurried. It made Rana smile just to watch him.

He was about to pass a narrow storefront when he stopped suddenly, head tilting toward a roughly drawn poster nailed to the frame. The image was crude, with chalky lines and smudged color, but clearly depicted small round spheres in a deep bowl. They almost looked like polished stones or fruit dipped in snow.

Intrigued, Rhyslin stepped inside.

Rana hesitated at first, then slipped in after him, the doorbell chiming faintly above her head. "What is it?" she asked, stepping up beside him.

Rhyslin gave a small shrug. "I do not know. Maybe we should ask him."

Her eyes followed his gaze to the man behind the counter. A Teine, plain in appearance, with short brown hair, a rust-colored shirt, and soft grey eyes. Friendly. But Rana didn't focus on his face for long. Her ears twitched. Her nose caught it first.

The smell was amazing.

Sweet. Cool. Almost intoxicating. She leaned toward the counter without meaning to, drawing in the layered scents. "Whatever it is," she whispered, "it smells good."

Rhyslin's brow arched slightly, curious. "What does it smell like?"

She closed her eyes for a moment, focusing. "Sùbh-lusan. Cherisean. Teòclaid. And... ùbhlan[3]." Her mouth began to water as her imagination raced ahead, painting flavors across her tongue. She could almost feel the texture, smooth, creamy, with that slight tart bite of fresh fruit. Her eyes fluttered open, wide and dilated.

Rhyslin turned back to the shopkeeper. "What are you selling?"

The man gave a proud little bow. "It's new. I call it *Iced Cream.*" The novelty of the name and the concept piqued their interest.

"Iced... cream?" Rhyslin echoed.

---

[3] Berries. Cherries. Chocolate. And... apples.

"I take creamed milk," the man explained, "cool it in my icehouse, and add bits of fresh fruit. Some like it plain, others want sweet sauces or shaved teòclaid. It's meant as a treat. Cold, sweet, and smooth."

Rana barely breathed as she listened. She'd never heard of such a thing. And yet... it sounded like exactly what she wanted.

Rhyslin didn't need to ask her. She stayed perfectly still, but her hope must have radiated like a beacon.

"I'd like two bowls," he said. "Teòclaid for me. Sùbh-lusan for the young lady."

The words made her chest flutter.

The vendor scooped two delicate servings into smooth clay bowls; each topped with a little flourish of crumbled topping. "For you, sir," he said, handing one to Rhyslin, "and for the lady."

Rana took hers carefully, inhaling the rich berry scent. It was almost too much. She waited long enough to see Rhyslin taste his and nod before lifting her own spoon.

The first bite sent a jolt through her mouth, cold, then warm with flavor. Sweetness laced with tartness; the richness of the cream offset by the wildness of fresh-picked sùbh-lusan. It melted across her tongue like snow-catching fire.

"Oh," she whispered. "This is good."

She devoured it slowly, savoring each bite, the tip of her tongue chasing the cold trail of sweetness from the spoon. Her eyes sparkled as she finished and placed the empty bowl gently back on the counter.

She turned toward Rhyslin, the corners of her mouth lifting with delight. "Thank you, Maighstir," she said, her voice soft but full of gratitude.

Rhyslin ate his bowl of cream more slowly than Rana, savoring the strange, smooth texture as it melted on his tongue. Cold at first, then rich with teòclaid, the flavor lingered like a childhood memory he hadn't lived. He hadn't tasted anything quite like it in all his years, not even in the high kitchens of Saorsa's capital or during his travels through the southern isles.

He set the empty bowl gently on the polished counter and gave the vendor a nod, offering a half-bow. "It is excellent. Thank you for the experience."

The man behind the counter beamed, clearly pleased. "I'm glad you enjoyed it. I make new batches every other day, takes about twelve uarian in the icehouse to freeze the crème right."

Rhyslin raised a brow at that. Twelve uarian. A delicate process, then. "How much do we owe you?"

"Five coppers per bowl," the man replied, holding up five fingers.

Rhyslin didn't hesitate. He pulled ten coppers from his pouch and dropped them into the man's waiting palm. "Worth every coin."

He turned to go but paused, casting a glance at Rana, who was still clutching her bowl like it contained some sacred elixir.

Her cheeks were faintly flushed, her eyes soft with contentment. It stirred something warm in his chest.

"If you can make extra," Rhyslin added, "I'll send for it in a few days."

The vendor nodded eagerly. "Of course, sir. Shall I prepare all four flavors?"

"Yes," Rhyslin replied, already picturing Ria's amused smirk and Flur's delighted hum as they tried it for the first time. "All four."

He stepped outside into the golden spill of the late afternoon sun, Rana following beside him. The air was still warm but with a soft undercurrent of coolness that whispered of the evening ahead. The scent of street spices and woodsmoke lingered on the breeze, mixing with the faint perfume of the wildflowers blooming in the baskets along the lampposts.

Rana walked close to him, a light bounce in her step, and for a long moment, neither of them spoke. Her happiness was palpable, quiet but sincere, and it soothed something in him that he hadn't known was restless.

Moments later, Marcus and Natolie rounded the corner, the ranger rubbing his belly with exaggerated reverence.

"I can't believe it tasted that good," Marcus said, reaching into his pouch and pulling out his pipe and leaf. "Do you think we could convince him to give us the recipe?"

Natolie's eyes lit with mischief. "We could *try*," she said, already scheming.

Rhyslin chuckled, withdrawing his own pipe and packing the minty leaf into the bowl. A small flicker of flame danced from his fingertips as he lit it.

He drew in slowly, the cool taste clearing his senses. "We'd need to ask Ria and Flur. But even then, I'm not sure our kitchen could replicate it. Some things," he said with a sidelong glance, "require magic that isn't just in the weave."

Rembran, Ixa, and Andros joined them shortly after; all three relaxed in that rare way soldiers get when the danger has passed but duty hasn't yet returned. Andros looked thoroughly pleased with himself, and Ixa was still licking a bit of teòclaid from her fingertip.

"What did you think, Rembran?" Rhyslin asked as the spell-blade stepped into the sun.

Rembran exhaled, pretending to fan away the smoke from Rhyslin's pipe. "It's a unique taste. And you're probably right, if your cooks try, they'll end up with chilled porridge."

Rhyslin laughed, genuine and deep in his chest. The simplicity of the moment, their laughter, the taste of something new, and the warmth of the sun were a balm.

"What now?" Rembran asked, stretching. "Are we heading back to the inn?"

Rhyslin looked toward Marcus, who gave a casual shrug.

"For now," the draoidh said. "Let's return to the Silver Moon. I have some tasks to finish before we leave, and the council may need us again, especially if that shadow beast resurfaces."

The moment sobered slightly at the reminder. But for now, the sweetness of the treat lingered, and as they began walking, Rhyslin allowed himself a rare thing.

Rana listened to the men talk, nodding in response to what they said. A playful smile danced across her lips as she teased Rhyslin. "You might not want to return right away. You slipped away without telling any of your cearcall goodbye."

The draoidh feigned fright and managed to fake a shiver. "Oh, the horror. My bannaichean might be upset with me." His eyes sparkled in mirth. "Whatever will I do to get back in their good graces?"

Rana pretended to think that over. "You might have to throw Flur over your shoulder and promise to spank her," she said deadpan.

Rhyslin, having already figured out Rana's wicked thoughts, nodded casually in agreement. "I could do the same to you, mo phrìseil."

"You keep threatening to do that," Rana grinned. "You're just afraid I'll bond with you if you push it too far." Even though her tone was light and playful, her body responded by tightening deliciously in anticipation.

As the draoidh watched Rana, he couldn't help but thinking that there was something wrong in the way women were treated. Almost as if they were afraid to admit to themselves the things they wanted most. When Rana shivered like she was anticipating his hands on her, he knew it was a good thing because the longer they spent in a healthy environment, the more they would admit what they wanted.

Rhyslin looked to where Natolie wrapped her arms around Marcus, cuddling close, whispering in his ears. Rhyslin couldn't hear what was said, though he could guess from Marcus' smug smile.

He didn't even have to look at Rembran. He could imagine that Ixa wrapped around the spell-blade like a blanket.

Instead of giving in to Rana's teasing, Rhyslin calmly replied. "My offer to bond with you remains open. All you need do is accept it." He had the satisfaction of seeing a slow blush crawl up Rana's throat.

Rana knew that she had two choices. She could

withdraw and hide her blush or stand brave and accept it for what it meant. She chose the second, lifting her head and staring into the draoidh's eyes. "You don't know what that means to me, Maighstir," she whispered as she moved to his side and took his free hand. She wondered if he would still want her after she had faced her doom.

Rhyslin gave Rana the comfort she sought, twining his fingers with her as they walked down the street. He could feel her happiness around her like a warm breeze.

The low murmur of conversation and the soft clink of mugs created a warm cocoon around the table. Flur leaned into the glow of the hearth fire, its flickering light casting golden shadows across the flagstone floor and dancing up the oak beams above. The scent of roasted chestnuts and sweet cider lingered in the air, wrapping around her like a memory.

Beside her, Ria was laughing, really laughing, the kind that made her eyes crinkle and her bond hum like music. Rowena, ever cool and composed, had just delivered a cutting remark that set Mayana sputtering into her tea, and even Allanagh, her mother, of all people, was chuckling with open mirth.

It felt like peace. Real peace. And Flur had no intention of breaking it. until the door opened. She turned automatically, following Ria's gaze, and her own heart jumped.

Rhyslin stood in the doorway, looking perfectly himself again,: alert, steady, a gentle strength radiating from him. But it wasn't just him. His hand was joined with Rana's, fingers loosely entwined, like the most natural thing in the world.

A quiet smile curved Ria's lips, her eyes shining with something softer than pride.

{*Welcome home, Maighstir mo Ghraidh,*} Ria said across the bond, her love curling gently around all of them.

Flur didn't speak aloud, either. She didn't have to.

{*Thank you for letting us sleep*}, she murmured into the bond, letting her affection flow freely. {*Rowena needed it bad*}, she added, unable to resist the teasing note.

The Mystic bristled across the link. {*I wasn't the one snoring like a Kree-beast,*} she replied archly, and the image of a shaggy desert lizard with a braid and a dramatic pillow sent a ripple of laughter through Flur and Ria both.

"I do *not* snore," Flur huffed aloud, tossing her braid over her shoulder for dramatic effect. She might have gotten away with it if not for the grin spreading across her mother's face.

"If you don't snore, Ithidh mi mo bhòtannan!4," Allanagh said, eyes gleaming with mischief. "I've heard sounds from your room at night that would scare off a banshee."

Flur's eyes widened, her hand flying to her chest in mock betrayal. "Mathair, how could you?" she gasped, aghast. "You swore you'd never use that against me."

"Oh, I swore no such thing," Allanagh said sweetly, sipping her drink like she hadn't just mortified her daughter in front of half the cearcall.

For a moment, Flur just stared, jaw slack, mortified, and then pointed a dramatic finger. "I will get you back for that."

Allanagh rolled her eyes, lifted her hand to her brow in theatrical despair, and let out a long, exaggerated sigh.

"Oh, the horror. My daughter is mad at me," she declared with mock woe. "How shall I ever cope?"

She delivered the line with such uncanny mimicry that Rana, who'd only just recovered from blushing earlier, clapped a hand over her mouth, trying not to burst.

Her shoulders shook with suppressed laughter until she finally gave up and pointed helplessly across the table.

"You sound exactly like Rhyslin did earlier!" she gasped between breathless giggles.

Allanagh blinked in confusion, then caught Rhyslin's raised brow and barely contained smirk. Recognition lit her eyes. "Oh no," she murmured in mock horror. "I've become him."

Rana lost it completely.

As her laughter echoed gently through the room, Flur caught Rhyslin's gaze, one brow arched. He gave her a small nod. Her lips curved just slightly, and she reached for her drink, visibly more at ease.

---

[4] I'll eat my boots.

The warmth at the table wrapped around them all, soft and familiar. The low light of the hearth threw golden shadows across the walls, and somewhere in the distance, a bard plucked a lazy tune on a lute.

Clearing her throat gently, Flur sat up straighter. "How long are we staying, Maighstir?" she asked, her voice still touched by laughter but steadied by intent. "Will we have time to shop for the house?"

Across the bond, Rhyslin felt her sincerity, not just about the logistics but about the life they were beginning to build. He nodded once.

"I was going to bring it up tomorrow with you and Ria," he said, his tone easy, open. "But since we're all here now, we can discuss it."

Ria leaned forward, her smile knowing. Rowena slid a seat out with one foot and gestured for Rhyslin to sit. As he did, Rana took the place beside him, still smiling faintly, her cheeks flushed from laughter.

The three bannaichean leaned in close, the firelight catching in their eyes, casting a soft glow on their faces. As the conversation turned toward furnishings, fabrics, and what color the sitting room curtains should be, Rana felt something settle quietly in her chest.

CHAPTER NINE

The Lesson of the Hands

The inn's common room was wrapped in a gentle quiet, a warm embrace before the dawn. Soft light seeped through the misted windows, casting a delicate golden hue on the stone floor. The hearth, a subdued glow, cast elongated shadows from the vacant chairs. Rhyslin reclined, his feet extended, one arm casually draped over the back of his seat. The weight of the night still lingered on his shoulders, but the tranquility of the silence was a soothing balm.

A clatter of footsteps broke the calm.

"What'll it be, Maighstir Darkblade?" the cook's assistant asked as she entered, tying her apron behind her back.

Her eyes twinkled when she saw him already half-draped in his seat.

Rhyslin stifled a yawn behind one hand. "Kafe, if there's any left. And something light to eat."

"Make that three," came Marcus's voice behind him.

Rhyslin glanced over as his friend stepped into the room, Natolie trailing just behind. She looked tired but at peace, her copper hair braided loosely over one shoulder. The moment she saw Rhyslin, she gave him a quiet, grateful smile and slid into the seat beside her husband.

"Three kafes and food, got it," the assistant grinned, already halfway to the kitchen. "You're lucky. The new bread just came out of the oven."

By the time the first steam-laced mugs arrived, Rhyslin had relaxed into the rhythm of the room, soft conversation, the occasional clink of ceramic, and the warm, bitter scent of roasted beans curling in the air.

Halfway through the meal, the door creaked open again.

"Mmm, that smells good," Flur murmured as she padded over, still wrapped in a loose robe, her hair tousled from sleep. She leaned down, arms circling Rhyslin's shoulders from behind. Her lips brushed the crown of his head.

"You're too good to us," came Ria's voice, soft and fond. She peered over Flur's shoulder, her dark hair spilling forward as she leaned in.

Rhyslin smiled, reaching back to rest a hand on Flur's forearm for a moment before he pushed his chair back just enough and reached up for Ria's hand. Ria blinked in mild surprise but didn't resist as he guided her into his lap.

The warmth of Rhyslin's body beneath hers was a quiet comfort, one she hadn't expected to crave so deeply. His lap was solid, grounding, like everything he was. She rested against him without protest, but her thoughts hummed beneath the surface.

She could feel Flur watching her. Ria turned just slightly, meeting her bond sister's sleepy gaze. Flur wrinkled her nose, then gave a small shrug, the kind that said *I love you, but I'm not getting up yet.*

Ria smiled faintly.

But her mind circled the same thought it had since she walked into the room: Rhyslin didn't rest, not really. He let all of them sleep in, yet he was always the first up. Always the one carrying everything.

She wanted to say it, to press her hand to his chest and tell him that she saw it, that he didn't have to keep doing it alone. But not in front of everyone. Not while Marcus and Natolie sipped their morning kafe, and Flur gnawed on a wedge of fruit, still wrapped in a blanket like a contented cat.

So, instead, she kept her voice light. "You keep letting us sleep, and we're going to get spoiled."

Rhyslin chuckled. *He knows.* She felt it through the bond like a thread of warmth coiling back toward her. "It's been a busy couple of weeks. You deserve it."

She shifted enough to look up at him, brushing her fingers lightly over his cheek. "You say that like you're not part of that 'we.' I haven't seen you sleep late even once."

His hand moved to her hip. "I don't need much sleep."

Typical. Stubborn. But not untrue. Ria could feel his strength thrumming low, like banked embers in a forge. He always ran hot, but even embers needed tending.

Before she could push further, he gently eased her from his lap and nudged his chair back. She gave a small sigh and settled into the seat beside him, pulling the warm mug toward her as the barmaid set it down. The steam curled into the air, fragrant with roasted beans and a touch of spice.

"What are we doing today?" she asked, cupping the mug between her hands.

He closed his eyes for a breath, and Ria watched him, always measured, always calculating. She knew the weight he carried, even when he made it look effortless.

"Other than going to the dockyard, I have little to do," he said at last, opening his eyes to meet hers.

Ria didn't respond right away. There was more she wanted to ask. *"Do you ever plan to rest? To let someone else carry the day?"*

Before she could find the words, Flur piped up from over his shoulder.

Flur's voice cut through the calm, her request hanging in the air like a promise. "Could we possibly have a healing lesson today?" she asked, plucking another piece of fruit from the plate between them, her eyes bright with anticipation.

Ria felt the shift in the room immediately, the slight straightening of Rhyslin's spine, the flicker of interest in his eyes.

The draoidh leaned back slightly in his chair, his eyes narrowing with quiet observation. "It would," he said, then turned his gaze toward Marcus. "Though speaking of healing, I noticed you've been favoring your right shoulder."

Marcus exhaled through his nose and rolled his eyes. "It's nothing," he muttered, rubbing at the spot instinctively. "Just muscle fatigue. Like you said, it's been a hard couple of weeks."

The attempt at levity didn't fool Rhyslin.

"I don't need to be your *Bhanna* to know that's a lie," he said dryly, the corner of his mouth quirking.

"If you will let me, I'll use you as our first lesson subject. I'd like to show Flur how to ease that tension properly."

Marcus grunted but nodded, his hand still resting on his shoulder. "Fine. I'm in your hands."

"You have my thanks," Rhyslin said with mock gravity. He turned his attention to Flur, who was already watching with a spark of eager curiosity lighting her blue eyes.

Rhyslin stood, only for Flur to nudge him gently with her elbow and a raised brow.

He sighed, then smirked. "Right. *After* we finish eating."

"I'm ready," Flur said as she gently pushed her plate forward, the scrape of ceramic on wood loud in the quiet of the inn's morning lull.

Her heart fluttered, not with fear but anticipation. Her blue eyes darted between Rhyslin and Marcus and back again, measuring, reading, hopeful.

Marcus groaned, long-suffering and dramatic, as he rubbed at the back of his neck. "Should've kept my mouth shut," he muttered, but there was no real heat behind the words. He slid his plate to the middle of the table with a grunt and slowly stood.

Flur noticed it. The small hitch in his breath. The subtle wince he tried to mask as he rolled his shoulder.

Rhyslin noticed, too.

"When did you hurt yourself, Marcus?" Rhyslin asked, his voice calm but threaded with concern.

Marcus waved it off with the same careless bravado he always wore like armor. "It's nothing. Just… muscle fatigue." But the pause was too long and the truth too thin.

Rhyslin's soft growl was more warning than rebuke. The sound made Flur's spine tingle. There was power in it and something protective, too.

"Okay, fine," Marcus relented, sighing. "During the battle at Tri Aibhnichean. I think I tweaked it when I was burying that Ogren with the others."

Flur frowned, her brows knitting together. That had been days ago. Weeks. She hadn't known he was still hurting.

"I'm sorry, old friend," Rhyslin said, something deeper flickering through his voice. Flur felt it echo across their bond, a quiet ache of guilt and care.

She stepped a little closer, standing straighter. "I'm ready to learn," she repeated, this time more softly.

Rhyslin turned to her and gave a small, warm nod. "Come, then. I'll show you how to take care of him."

Flur couldn't help the tiny smile that curled at her lips. She was ready for this, not just for the lesson, but to *help* someone. To touch that part of Rhyslin's world that was so often just his.

"What can I do?" Ria asked gently from the table.

Flur glanced back, watching as their dark-haired bond-sister looked up at Rhyslin with quiet affection. She knew what Ria meant, how easily Rhyslin gave of himself, how rarely he took rest.

"Stay here and enjoy your breakfast," he said with a smile. "Rana and Rowena should be down soon."

As they rose, Rhyslin slipped an arm around Flur's waist, grounding her in that quiet, familiar way of his. She leaned into his touch. Not because she needed to but because she wanted to.

Marcus was already heading toward the stairs, his footsteps slow but sure. Flur followed, her bare feet whispering against the wood, her heart beating a little faster with each step.

At the top, they paused for a moment as another couple descended, laughing softly, their hands brushing.

Rhyslin heard a grunt behind him and glanced over his shoulder to see Marcus wince in pain. *Here's hoping that Rana and Rowena are awake.* He paused at the door to his suite and slowly pushed it open to see Rowena slip into the second bedroom.

The morning light crept through the window, painting long amber streaks across the inn's wooden floor. It was early enough that the world outside still felt quiet, held in a breath between dreams and day. Rana sat curled on the window bench, her knees tucked beneath her and an old history tome spread open across her lap.

The pages smelled faintly of ink and pressed herbs, like something half-forgotten and sacred.

She didn't look up as Rhyslin entered; she didn't need to. She felt his presence in the same way she felt warmth on her skin after walking into sunlight.

"Good morning, Maighstir," she said lightly, tracing a line of old script with one finger. "I'm just waiting for Cailleach[5] to get dressed."

From the other room, Rowena's voice drifted out like a breeze full of dry laughter. "Some of us sleep late, dearling. We don't all leap out of bed with the unnatural energy of the young and overachieving."

Rana smirked and tilted her head just enough to call back, "You mean some of us take an hour to pick a shirt."

There was a soft thud of a cabinet closing, then the whisper of footsteps before Rowena emerged. She looked effortlessly put together, hair swept into a loose braid that somehow made her look both noble and untouchably serene. Her blouse was tucked just so, though she still fussed with the hem as she crossed the room to the mirror.

Rana watched her out of the corner of her eye as Rowena, although not much older than Rana, but just a touch more mature, examined her reflection, adjusting a strand of hair and letting out a breath.

"Not perfect," Rowena sighed to herself, "but it'll have to do."

---

[5] Old hag, old woman

Then she turned, eyes sharp and amused. "Come along, Fiadh beag, let's go eat."

Rana blinked. *Fiadh beag?* Little deer? She frowned for a second, unsure if she was being mocked or gently teased. Probably both, if she knew Rowena, and she was starting to. The older woman had a knack for insults that somehow felt like compliments in disguise.

Rana gave her an exaggerated shrug and snapped the book closed. "I'm still deciding if I like that nickname."

Rowena arched a brow as if to say *you will* and then turned for the door with the kind of grace that made even the inn's worn floorboards seem refined.

Rana slid off the bench and followed her footsteps soft behind the swish of Rowena's skirt.

Something was comforting in the rhythm of their steps, like the way she and her mother used to walk together back in the desert. Back before, everything changed.

As they stepped into the hallway, the scent of hearth fire and rising bread reached her, and for the first time that morning, Rana realized she was actually hungry.

Rhyslin kissed his Mystic softly, savoring the warmth of her lips before she swept out of the room. The door clicked shut behind her, and he turned to Marcus with a raised brow.

"You know what to do," he said.

Marcus grunted, pulling off his shirt with a wince. "Yeah, yeah. I should've kept my mouth shut."

He slumped into the nearest chair, twisting it around so he could lean his chest against the back. The wood creaked in protest.

Rhyslin watched him settle. Sunlight filtered through the curtains in dappled patterns, catching the pale scars that crisscrossed Marcus's back. "You can have your patient lie on the bed or a table," he explained to Flur, gesturing casually. "But for now, we'll keep our ranger right where he is. He's grumpier when he's horizontal."

Flur leaned closer, studying the web of scars etched across Marcus's back. Some were clean, others jagged, as if stitched in haste or not at all.

"He's got so many scars," she murmured, voice caught between awe and worry. "How can you even tell where he hurts?"

"You ask him," Rhyslin replied, his tone laced with mild amusement. "Or, if he won't answer, you prod until he growls."

The draoidh stepped behind Marcus, laying his fingertips along the ranger's shoulder with practiced ease. "Each bone has two muscle groups attached. They tighten or loosen depending on the movement. It's your job to listen with your hands."

Flur followed his lead, gently running her fingers across the curve of the collarbone. The skin was warm, ridged with old battles. "This doesn't feel right. He's not reacting."

"Then move down his back. Look for tension. A knot. A flinch," Rhyslin said. "Or better yet, if he'd admit when he's in pain. But Marcus?" He chuckled. "He'd rather chew gravel."

"Stick it, you old coot," Marcus growled. He tensed and winced when she pressed a little harder near his scapula. "Damnit, woman, not so hard."

"Stop being such a pàisde[6]" she shot back, pressing more gently as her fingers searched for the source of tension. The muscle beneath her hand twitched slightly. "He's got a knot, I think."

"Hmm?" Rhyslin stepped in, placing his fingers beside hers, his touch confident and sure. Marcus growled again, though more under his breath than anything else.

"Don't make me muzzle you, old wolf," Rhyslin muttered.

Marcus quieted, but his posture remained taut. Flur brushed a loose lock of golden hair behind her ear as she looked up.

"What now?"

"Now, we work to release the knot," Rhyslin said calmly. "Apply pressure. Circle left, then right."

Flur nodded and pressed down with care, circling as instructed. The knot resisted at first, then slowly gave under her touch. Marcus sighed, the sound soft but filled with relief.

"Like that?"

"Exactly," Rhyslin confirmed. "Once that one releases, keep going. You'll find more."

---

[6] baby

Her confidence grew with each movement. She worked her way down Marcus's back, searching for and unraveling tight spots. When he grunted again, she smirked.

"For such an old wolf, you're acting more like a cuilean ùr-bhreith[7]," she teased.

"You're doing a good job," Marcus admitted through clenched teeth, "but it still hurts."

Rhyslin, overhearing, leaned in once more, his brow furrowing. "If the massage isn't working, then it may not be a knot. You might have bruised the bone or cracked it."

That made Flur pause. Her fingers hovered.

"In that case," Rhyslin added gently, "we'll need help. Mathair's help. How are your prayers these days?"

Flur glanced down, suddenly uncertain. "Okay, I guess. Not very poetic."

Rhyslin gave her a knowing smile. "Mathair doesn't care for poetry. She prefers honesty. Ask her the way you'd ask your own mother."

---

[7] Newborn puppy

Flur took a breath. Her hand trembled slightly as she laid it over the injured spot. Her voice was quiet but steady.

"Mathair, this poor old wolf has hurt himself. Would you please help me fix him?"

At her side, Rhyslin hid a knowing smile behind his hand as Flur whispered her prayer.

Marcus's eyes widened. *Fix me? Ifrinn, no.* "Hey! I'm not some dog that …" he muttered, but his protest stalled when warmth bloomed under Flur's palm, gentle and radiant, like sunlight melting frost. He took a deep breath as the pain slipped away.

"Ah… yes. Right there," Marcus whispered, his eyes fluttering shut. "Thank you, Mathair."

When he opened them again, Flur was watching him with a soft, proud smile. "Thank you, Flur," he added, then grimaced slightly. "Did you have to phrase it *that* way?"

Flur giggled and swatted his good shoulder. "That's what you get for snapping at your healer."

Suitably chastened, Marcus grumbled something unintelligible.

Flur tilted her head. "I didn't quite hear that," she teased.

"I'm sorry," he mumbled. "I shouldn't have snapped like that."

Forgiven, Flur thought, though she let the silence stretch just long enough to make him sweat a little.

CHAPTER TEN

Breadth of Sky and Bow of Ship

Marcus descended the stairs with careful, measured steps, his heart buoyed by the absence of the sharp twinge and stiffness that had plagued him for days.

Rhyslin looked up from the open window, pipe in hand, and arched a brow. "You're looking better."

Marcus gave a noncommittal grunt, half a smile playing at the corners of his mouth as he crossed the common room. He joined Rhyslin at the window, lighting his own pipe with a practiced flick. The sweet, loamy scent of the mint leaf curled in his lungs, not quite strong enough to drown the city stench outside, sour sewage, hot stone, and too many people packed too close together.

The distant sound of a street performer's flute added a touch of whimsy to the otherwise grim atmosphere.

He exhaled a slow stream of smoke. "I can finally move it again," he muttered, rolling his shoulder. *Thank the gods and Flur's gentle hands.*

Rhyslin gave him a once-over, eyes twinkling. "I can't believe you repaid Flur's devotion by snapping at her."

Marcus groaned, his hand rubbing his face in mock exasperation. "You're never going to let me live that down, are you?" he teased.

"I'm not the one you growled at," Rhyslin shot back, all mock innocence. "I'm just the one who witnessed it. But you have to admit, it was quite a sight."

Their banter, a familiar form of camaraderie, lightened the heavy air in the room.

Of course, he was enjoying this. Marcus sighed and cast a sidelong look at his friend. "You're evil."

The draoidh pretended to be scandalized. "Evil? Me? A' Mathair would be heartbroken to hear you say such a thing about her favorite son."

Marcus snorted. "Pretty sure you got dropped on your head as a babe."

Rhyslin shrugged. "But it's still been far too long since I've had the upper hand in our banter. I intend to savor this."

Marcus raised both hands in surrender, pipe clamped between his teeth. "Fine. You win. You happy now?"

Rhyslin puffed thoughtfully before responding. "Immensely."

They stood in companionable silence for a moment, the morning sunlight stretching long golden beams across the wooden floor, broken only by the murmur of voices from the street and the occasional creak of shifting timber.

Marcus shifted his gaze outside, his eyes bright with anticipation as he watched a merchant cart bump along the cobbles. "So, are we still checking out that new ship of yours?" he asked, his voice filled with the thrill of the unknown.

"I thought we might," Rhyslin said, eyes unreadable.

Marcus gave him a sidelong look. "You've got

that tone again. The one that means you're up to something."

A faint smirk curved Rhyslin's mouth. "Maybe. You got something else in mind?"

"Besides getting out of this gods-forsaken city?" Marcus grimaced. "I'd rather go toe-to-toe with that shadow creature again than breathe another day of sewer steam."

Rhyslin laughed, his exhale mingling with the city air. "If the *Cloud Dancer* is ready, we can leave today. I've got Rembran and the others on standby." He gestured toward the trio across the room, Rembran leaning into a quiet conversation with Ixa and Andros, the air around them filled with easy familiarity.

Marcus knocked the ash from his pipe against the window ledge. "Did you tell Flur and Ria about the iced cream?"

Rhyslin shook his head, and the gleam in his eyes turned mischievous. "No. Thought I'd let that be a surprise."

Marcus chuckled low in his throat. "You know you've already set the bar pretty high for favorite cearcall member, right?"

"I don't compete with my own bannaichean," Rhyslin replied, puffing again on his pipe. "I just give them reasons to love me."

Marcus rolled his eyes. "You're impossible."

"And yet," Rhyslin said with mock humility, "you still follow me around."

The ranger couldn't help it. He grinned despite the city stench. despite the headache of the past few days. "Yeah, well. Someone's got to stick a pin in that swelling ego of yours."

Rhyslin looked toward the door as a deep voice echoed through the common room, tinged with the early clang of the inn's bell as someone stepped inside. The familiar cadence made him smile before the man from last night strode in, eyes sweeping the room until they landed on him.

"Maighstir Darkblade," the merchant called, his voice warm and booming as he gestured behind him. A second man followed; shoulders hunched under the weight of two wide-lidded containers. "I have your delivery."

Rhyslin inclined his head in greeting, pipe smoke curling lazily from his lips. From the table across the room, he saw three eyes lift in unison. Flur's expression was already bright with curiosity, and a moment later, she leaned over to whisper something to Ria. The two women shared a glance thick with mischief and wordless understanding. Rowena didn't need to ask. She simply nodded, rising smoothly with them.

Here it comes, Rhyslin thought, hiding his grin.

The three walked across the room with all the solemn intent of an inquisition, if the inquisition wore silk and moved like a breeze through a flower field. Flur leaned over his shoulder, her golden hair brushing against his arm.

"What is this?" she asked, blue eyes narrowing at the containers.

Rhyslin adopted an innocent tone. "This? Just something I thought you might enjoy."

Ria raised an eyebrow, arms crossed. Her expression dared him to keep up the charade.

"Did you bring the samples as well?" Rhyslin asked the merchant, still feigning ignorance.

"Yes, sir. As requested, three of each flavor." The man smiled and nodded politely to the three approaching women.

Rhyslin motioned to the table. "Ladies, if you would?" They sat without hesitation, curiosity radiating from all three as they eyed the covered bowls. "This is iced cream," he explained. "If you like it, I'll see about keeping a few containers on hand." He turned to the merchant. "Have your assistant take the large containers to the cold room."

"Of course, sir," the merchant said. He turned toward the innkeeper. "Will it be an imposition, Paole?"

"Not at all," Paole replied, gesturing to the back room.

Rhyslin watched as the assistant followed instructions, then turned back to the table just as the merchant began uncovering the small sample bowls. Sweet, cool scents immediately wafted into the air.

"That smells so good," Flur murmured, already leaning forward.

Ria's nostrils flared delicately. "Choca and sùbh-lusan," she guessed, eyes fluttering closed for a moment as she inhaled. "Are you sure this is safe?"

Rhyslin smirked. "Rana adored it. I wouldn't dare speak for you, though."

Ria shot him a look that promised payment later.

Then, like a cat testing cream, she dipped her spoon into the dessert and tasted it.

Flur beat her to it. She took a generous bite, eyes going wide as the flavors hit. "This is *amazing*," she moaned.

Rhyslin nearly choked on a laugh.

Ria tried her own spoonful, and her eyes closed with a slow exhale. "It's like frozen joy."

He chuckled as all three women dug in.

"Can we have this delivered regularly?" Flur asked, wiping her lips and giving him a pleading look.

Ria leaned into his side. "If it stays frozen long enough to make the trip, I'd say it's worth every coin."

Rhyslin nodded to the merchant. "We'll take what you brought today. Ria will handle payment."

The merchant glanced at Ria, who was still licking her spoon with practiced elegance. Her smile was razor-sharp and entirely pleased.

"Of course, sir. I'll be in touch about regular shipments."

Rhyslin leaned down, brushing a kiss against Ria's ear. Her breath hitched, her body practically melting against him.

"Would you mind? Marcus and I need to check on the new ship. I'm taking Rana."

"Mmm," she purred, eyes half-lidded. "I'll pay him. But if you keep doing things like this, you're going to owe me more than iced cream."

He grinned, brushing his fingers along her jaw before stepping back. She whimpered just once.

Flur was watching them both with her spoon paused mid-air. "You two are impossible."

"Delightfully so," Rhyslin said.

With a final glance, more of a warning, really, he caught Marcus's attention and tilted his head toward the door. Time to go before Ria decided she wanted dessert of another kind.

Rhyslin brushed a final kiss across Rowena's lips, savoring the dazed look it left on her face and turned toward the door. As he passed Flur, he let his hand sweep affectionately across her lower back, eliciting a smoldering glance that promised more if they weren't headed out. Their bond shimmered with restrained heat.

Then, pausing beside Rana, he leaned close, his breath teasing her ear. "Let's take a walk."

She beamed, lips twitching with suppressed joy, and fell in step beside him.

Outside, the city greeted them with a gust of late-morning wind. The streets pulsed with life: merchants hawking fresh bread and salted fish, children weaving between carts, and the occasional clang of a hammer from the dockyards in the distance. Rhyslin exhaled slowly, letting the chaotic rhythm of urban life wash over him.

Marcus and Natolie followed at a cautious distance, the ranger's gaze sweeping alleys and balconies for threats. Behind them came Rembran, Ixa practically glowing at his side, and Andros bringing up the rear, his heavy footfalls steady as drumbeats.

"Where are we off to, Rhys?" Marcus asked, eyeing a cluster of beggars nestled near the baker's stall.

"The Cloud Dancer," Rhyslin replied, swinging his staff over his shoulder. "She might be ready."

Ixa's eyes lit like twin suns. "And if she is?"

"We take her for a spin. Then, if she handles well, we bring her home to finish outfitting."

Rembran matched his grin. "How long's it been?"

"Six months," Rhyslin said, tipping his hat against the wind as it tried to tug it loose. The breeze danced through the avenue, scattering leaves and lifting the scent of distant sea salt and chimney smoke.

Rana skipped up beside him. "What kind of ship is the Cloud Dancer?"

"Cutter. Thirty-six feet bow to stern. Twenty-foot beam. Crew of sixty-six."

Rembran's voice dropped to reverent awe. "And she flies like a moonbeam."

Rhyslin chuckled. "She's yours, if you think you can manage her."

Rembran blinked. "Me, sir?"

Rhyslin nodded. "Captain's cabin included. Andros gets the room beside it. Ixa stays too."

The spell-blade glanced at Ixa with hope plain on his face. She squeezed his hand in answer.

"Are you ready for this?" Rhyslin asked Andros.

"Oh yes," the earth elemental said, grinning.

But Ixa's voice dropped. "We're still mad at you."

Rhyslin looked at her, brow raised.

"You shut your mind to us, let us scream in the dark."

"And when Rembran gave us form," Andros added, his tone gentler now, "I got to fight. To be grounded again. It helped."

Ixa's cheeks flushed with heat. "And the chains helped too," she said shyly, glancing up at Rembran.

Rembran's smile curled. "As did the silken veils."

He turned to Rhyslin. "You were there. Who chose their attire? Them or me?"

Rhyslin exhaled thoughtfully. "The Other world pulls from the minds present. Likely a bit of both."

He turned his gaze on Ixa. "What did you think when you found yourself in chains?"

The blush deepened, climbing down her throat. "That it felt... like something a caileag-thraille might wear." Her voice was barely above a whisper. "And I wondered what it would be like to be presented in silks. For him."

Rhyslin arched a brow. "And how did it feel?"

Ixa leaned into Rembran's side. "At first, I was furious. Then he used my power, broke the enemy with it. I wanted to please him. I still do." She stood on tiptoe and brushed a kiss against Rembran's cheek.

The spell blade's eyes glittered with something deeper than pride. He said nothing, but his hand curved around her waist, protective and claiming all at once.

Natolie leaned in toward Marcus, her words too soft to catch. Whatever she whispered made the ranger's mouth twitch, and he gave a slow nod. She slipped her hand into his, her fingers curling with practiced familiarity.

Just ahead, Ixa turned her head over her shoulder, her eyes alight with mischief. "It wouldn't take but a breath for me to slip into those silks again," she purred at Rembran.

The spell-blade's expression didn't change, but his palm landed with a sharp, open-handed swat to her backside. The soft *crack* echoed faintly along the stone-paved street.

Ixa gasped, eyes wide, lips parted in a perfect O, as a shiver danced down her spine. She melted into Rembran's side, a hushed, breathless, "Yes, Maighstir. I'll behave," escaping her lips as she clutched his arm.

Rana bit back a laugh, watching with both amusement and growing curiosity. Ixa's reaction was theatrical but honest. Her whole body hummed with pleasure, and Rana couldn't help but wonder what that kind of surrender might feel like.

CHAPTER ELEVEN

Stench and Summons

Rana had barely taken two steps before she caught the low sigh Rhyslin released. Something about it made her chest tighten. A half-step more, and she smelled it too, sour, rotten like fruit left too long in the sun.

Then came the squelch.

She glanced down just in time to see Rhyslin lift his left boot, a trail of brown sludge clinging to the sole. His expression soured, the corners of his lips curling in disgust as he sidestepped a pile of refuse. The air around them was thick with the mingling stench of decay and sewage. Not even the faint ocean breeze could cut through it.

This wasn't what she'd imagined a capital city would be.

Without thinking, she skipped a step and slid her hand into Rhyslin's. His palm was warm, calloused. Grounding. "What's wrong, Maighstir?" she asked softly.

He shook his head. "It's nothing, really."

She didn't believe him for a second.

"Which of your rules are you about to break?" she asked with sly innocence.

Rhyslin stumbled. Not physically, but in that subtle way where she felt the hitch in his stride through their joined hands. She bit back a grin.

He didn't answer.

Rana halted abruptly, her skirts flaring slightly with the motion. She dug in her heels just enough to pull him a half-step off balance, forcing him to brace with his staff.

He turned toward her, brows lifted in faux surprise. "Yes?"

Rana stood, hands on her hips. She arched one brow. "Are you going to answer my question or not?"

Rather than deflect, he gestured at the street. "Take a look around. Tell me what you see."

She did. She saw narrow streets littered with waste, the stone stained from years of foot traffic and discarded meals. The buildings rose high on either side, casting long shadows that made even midday feel dim. Alley mouths yawned like hungry maws, dark and uninviting.

"I see a city that stinks," she said bluntly. "Claustrophobic. Ugly. Smothering."

He nodded slowly, something like sorrow passing through his eyes. "That's not how Marcus and I designed it."

She blinked. "You what?"

Rhyslin resumed walking, and she scrambled to fall in step beside him. "You helped design this place?"

"We tried to make it beautiful," he said, his voice distant. "Wide avenues paved in brick. Courtyards shared between buildings. Green groves every few blocks. Marcus and I modeled it after the old imperial cities."

"So… what happened?"

"Greed," came Marcus' voice, blunt as always. He and Natolie stepped up beside them, their boots crunching against loose gravel. "Long blocks and narrow streets mean more buildings. More rent. More profit."

Rana looked at him, appalled. "Couldn't you have made them follow your plan?"

Rhyslin gave a small, sad smile. "That's not how liberty works."

"But you had the council. The army."

"And we weren't tyrants," he replied, his voice firm now. "We didn't build the Saorsa so we could become what we once overthrew."

Rana fell silent, absorbing that. She thought of the crown he'd refused at Tri Aibhnichean, the day he'd turned victory into peace.

Up ahead, the wind shifted. It stirred dust from the cobbles, and with it came the sharp scent of movement.

Rana stopped. "Someone's coming," she warned, her head tilting instinctively. She closed her eyes, focusing. Boots. Five or six. Coming fast.

Rhyslin reacted instantly. He gave a sharp gesture to Marcus and Rembran, who fanned out with Natolie, Ixa, and Andros to form a loose semi-circle behind them.

Rana sniffed again.

She knew that scent.

She hissed, voice low. "Maighstir... it's Lieutenant Sparhawk."

Rana stiffened as soon as she caught the cadence of the approaching boots. Four of them. Heavy, armored, measured. Her ears caught the subtle scrape of chain mail over gambeson before her eyes did.

From the shadows at the end of the street, a figure emerged, sharp, angular, confident. Even before she saw his face, she knew who it was.

Sparhawk.

At her side, Rhyslin muttered something low and dark under his breath. She heard it clearly: "What does he want now?"

The draoidh leaned on his staff, unreadable. Beside her, Marcus subtly shifted, hand brushing his hip as if confirming the familiar weight of his weapons. Natolie had already turned slightly, weight balanced on the balls of her feet. Ixa and Andros fell quiet, attentive.

As the soldier and his three companions approached, the street narrowed under the press of tension. Rhyslin didn't move, didn't blink.

"I see you, Lieutenant Sparhawk," he called, his voice calm and precise. "You may approach."

Sparhawk's armor clinked softly as he deliberately stepped forward. When he stopped just shy of the protective semi-circle they'd formed, his eyes found her immediately. Not Rhyslin. Her.

Rana straightened, eyes narrowing.

"Maighstir Darkblade," Sparhawk said with a courteous half-bow.

Then he turned to her.

"Boidhchead le spuirean."

Rana blinked, parsing the words. Beauty with claws. Her lips twitched. She *liked* that.

A slow, amused smile curled on her lips as she returned a half-curtsy, fluid and mocking. "Fear fiadhaich le sgaraidhean," she replied, her tone silken. Wildman with scars.

The faintest glint of white teeth showed in Sparhawk's expression.

"Maighstir Darkblade," he continued, breaking the moment between them. "The council requests your presence when you have a moment."

Rana sensed Marcus tense again at her side. "I thought the council adjourned until the next session," he said, voice cool. "What do they want now?"

Sparhawk rubbed his thumb across one of the scars on his left cheek, a habit Rana had begun to recognize as nerves cloaked in control.

"They didn't tell me why," he admitted. "But I overheard a sagart speaking with General Oberon. Something about San Ang's monastery. They haven't heard from them in some time."

Rana exchanged a glance with Rhyslin, her heart skipping a beat. Not from fear. From knowing. That kind of silence rarely meant anything good.

"I see," Rhyslin said at last.

Rana watched him carefully, memorizing the subtle hardening in his posture and the way his hand wrapped more tightly around his staff. Whatever was waiting in San Ang had already begun to ripple through the weave. And she had a feeling they'd be heading into it soon.

The stink hit Sparhawk full in the face like a rotten fist.

One moment, he was standing at the edge of the group, catching his breath; the next, he was gagging quietly behind his closed mouth, the stench of wet feces rising from the sewer grates like something dead and clinging. His tongue went thick with it, and he fought the instinct to spit, settling instead for shallow breaths through his mouth. Even that barely helped.

I hate this city, he thought grimly. *Give me an open field, a patrol in the wilds, hells, even a flooded trench, just not this cesspool masquerading as a capital.*

He shifted his weight subtly and caught movement in the corner of his eye. Lieutenant Sparhawk spit to the side with a low, disgusted curse.

"By Mixcoatl, that's foul," Marcus grunted, nostrils flaring as he tried to clear them. "I hope that cutter is finished so we can get out of here."

Sparhawk murmured a wordless agreement. His gaze drifted toward the one bright spot in the grimy street: Rana.

The young spell blade stood just ahead, her face turned slightly toward the wind. She was clearly struggling against the same nauseating stench, her bronze skin gone a shade paler, jaw clenched tight. For all that, she didn't complain. She simply endured, chin lifted, back straight, like a flame refusing to bow before the wind.

His gaze lingered on her hazel eyes, flecked with gold. Her raven hair tumbling over her shoulder.

Lithe form wrapped in her simple, elegant dress. She was unlike anyone he'd met. Wild. Sharp. Beautiful.

You can't possibly be infatuated with a prey species, he told himself, already hating the thought. But when Rana's eyes flicked to meet his bright, intelligent, unflinching, he felt the heat crawl up the back of his neck.

He didn't even hear the draoidh until his name was spoken.

"Lieutenant Sparhawk."

He blinked as he was yanked out of his thoughts. Rhyslin's voice was calm, but with that undercurrent of command that always made Sparhawk stand straighter.

"Sir?" He cleared his throat and snapped to attention.

"Would you be so kind as to find Oberon and tell him we'll meet him in two hours?" Rhyslin said, the staff in his hand thudding softly against the cobblestones. "Gather your squad and meet us at the barracks."

"Yes, sir." Sparhawk placed a fist to his heart, saluting with discipline. Then, hesitantly, he extended his arm toward Rhyslin. "Sir, why do you want my squad?"

He winced internally. *Stupid. Don't question the draoidh in front of others.*

But Rhyslin didn't flare or frown. Instead, he raised a brow, calm, unreadable.

"Is something wrong with your squad?" Marcus asked, voice cool but curious.

"No, sir," Sparhawk replied quickly, standing taller. "I'm just… surprised. We didn't exactly start off on the right foot."

Understanding bloomed behind Rhyslin's eyes.

"Ah. I don't hold mistakes against people," the draoidh said. "If I did, Rembran would still be a pilot trainee."

Rembran chuckled under his breath at that, and Sparhawk felt the knot in his chest loosen slightly.

"Depending on what we find at the monastery," Rhyslin continued, "it could get bad quickly."

"Besides," Marcus added with a wry grin, "being out there is better than being here."

Sparhawk didn't argue. The smell alone was reason enough.

"Understood, sir. I'll meet you at the hall in two hours." He gave one final nod, then turned on his heel.

He didn't glance back at Rana, but her eyes stayed with him the whole way down the street.

Rana waited until Sparhawk's squad vanished around the corner before she turned to Rhyslin. Her question was soft but thoughtful. "What is San Ang's Monastery? Is it important?"

Rhyslin didn't answer right away. His eyes drifted toward the horizon as a bitter gust stirred the reeking refuse along the edge of the street. The sharp, sour scent of rot stung his nostrils. He almost didn't notice it. Almost.

But it layered over everything in Aus town now, a reminder of what it had become.

He let out a breath, quiet and heavy. "Angus McReady was a ridere who followed He Who Watches. He built a saor-shealbh a decade after the founding of Saorsa, a small refuge. He spent years defending the frontier against Orcan, Ogren, and Na-Thuit raids. Even crossed into Bazan when needed."

The words burned like the taste of ash. Rhyslin paused, feeling the grime of the city clinging to his skin like a second coat. A waft of rotten fruit drifted through the air, and his stomach turned.

"During one raid, he was captured by an Ogren and tortured for weeks. Even under the worst of it, he never renounced his faith. When his men rescued him, he was broken but unbent. He lived another twenty years, always in pain. Before he died, he converted his home into a place of healing. A sanctuary for old soldiers."

Rhyslin felt his throat catch, so Marcus took over smoothly.

"When he passed, he left it to the Order of the Lily," Marcus said, his voice quieter than usual. "They've cared for it ever since."

Rembran stepped in, speaking with reverence. "They expanded the grounds. Last census, there were about eight hundred old soldiers there. Two hundred staff, hearth-maidens, battle priests, healers, and clerics."

Rhyslin nodded. His fingers trembled slightly. He called on the rune, a simple trace in the air with one fingertip. Blood answered.

It welled from his nose unbidden, falling in six perfect droplets to the cobblestones, arranging themselves in a spiral glyph. The air seemed to still.

He whispered, "What do you mean, gin?"

He repeated the rune, slower this time. Again, the blood obeyed.

"Tha," he murmured, his voice ragged. He pressed a hand over his heart, the gesture instinctive. Something was wrong. Deeply wrong.

He turned to Marcus. "We need to get to the monastery. As soon as possible."

His hands shook. His soul did, too. The glyph glistened at his feet, a warning written in blood. And he feared he already knew what it meant.

Marcus exchanged a silent look with Rhyslin, then nodded. "Let's get to the construction yard and see if that cutter's done," he said, pivoting sharply on his heel.

The stink of the city clung to his nostrils, wet refuse, piss, something acrid that might have once been food. Ause City was rotting from the inside out, he thought grimly. With every step, he tried not to breathe too deeply.

Halfway down the street, a high-pitched cry echoed above them. Marcus paused and tilted his head toward the sky. A shadow circled once, then dove with swift precision. He raised his left arm just as the red-banded hawk flared her wings and landed neatly. Her talons gripped his bracer as she stepped up to perch on his shoulder. With a soft chirrup, she leaned forward and touched her beak to his ear.

The moment their heads connected, his vision dimmed, replaced by flickering images: dead auroch and horses, unnatural strains of mold and fungus around them. Something primal stirred in him, something that hadn't surfaced since the War of Bones. He blinked, then turned to Rhyslin. "You'll have to go to San Ang's without me. I'm needed on the ranges. Something strange has happened."

Rhyslin stepped forward, his expression unreadable. "Is that Cabhlach Sgiath?"

Marcus nodded once. "She wouldn't have come otherwise."

The draoidh held out his right hand. The hawk considered him for a moment, then dipped her head beneath his palm. Marcus felt the shift the instant Rhyslin connected.

The air pulsed faintly around them as if time itself stilled. When Rhyslin pulled away, his face had gone pale.

"Yes," he murmured. "You're needed. We'll drop you and Natolie off on the way to the manse."

Marcus glanced at his wife, who had already stepped forward, calm and ready as ever. "Good. And I'll take Angelica and Damien with me. Damien could use some time away from the scrolls."

Rhyslin nodded in agreement, but when he said he'd be taking Rana with him, Marcus wasn't surprised to see the girl shake her head with a smirk. "Flur won't let you leave her behind," she said, amused. "Momma and Rowena might want to stay, but not her."

They left the choking stench of the alleyways behind and stepped out into a wide, open field that stretched like a balm before them. Marcus inhaled deeply, gratefully. Wild grasses rustled in the breeze. The sun warmed his shoulders.

"Thank Mixcoatl," he muttered, shoulders easing for the first time in hours. "Go check on your cutter, I'm staying here."

Rhyslin gave a tired chuckle. "Just getting above the stink would be worth it."

Ahead, the black iron gates of the shipyard stood half-open. Beyond them, the broad yard stretched toward a series of warehouses and work sheds. A framework of scaffolding cast narrow shadows on the gravel.

Marcus stopped just outside the gate, settling against the wall. "Nat and I will wait out here."

The others passed through one by one, their steps lighter in the cleaner air. Even Rana, who had paused to savor the sunlight like a cat warming itself on a window ledge, soon fell into step beside Rhyslin.

Marcus leaned his head back and closed his eyes. The hawk shifted slightly on his shoulder, and for a moment, all was still.

He knew the peace wouldn't last long, not with San Ang's monastery gone silent and darkness creeping over the horizon. But for now, he breathed in the quiet and let the clean air fill his lungs.

The moment Rana passed through the iron gates beside Rhyslin, the sound hit her like a thunderclap. The wall wasn't to keep people out. It was to keep the chaos in.

She staggered as the cacophony rolled over her. Hammers rang out in staccato rhythms, sawblades shrieked like dying spirits, and harsh voices barked over one another. The very air seemed to vibrate with noise. Her ears throbbed. Whimpering, she clapped her hands over them and ducked her head, trying to escape the onslaught.

Then the sawdust hit. A swirl of grit rushed into her mouth and nose. She choked, coughing hard enough that her knees buckled.

Warmth steadied her.

Rhyslin.

He said nothing, just handed her a length of soft homespun cloth from one of his pouches. She blinked through tears at him until he gently showed her how to wrap it around her head, covering her ears, her mouth, and her nose.

The moment she tucked it into place, some of the pressure eased. Her breath came easier. She rested her forehead and hands against Rhyslin's chest, anchoring herself against the thunder of laboring men and machines.

He wrapped one arm around her shoulders, fingers stroking lightly along her spine. The sound dimmed to something manageable. Her heart, still fluttering like a bird, began to slow.

"Is it always this loud?" she whispered up at him.

"It is," he replied softly, his voice threading through the chaos like balm. "I'm sorry. Do you want to wait outside with Marc and Nat?"

Rana shook her head, hair sliding against the cloth like a river of ink. "No," she said with a breathless laugh. "I'll stay with you… unless you tell me to leave."

He studied her, and she could feel it even with her eyes closed. The warmth of his gaze was its own kind of sunlight. When she opened her eyes, his smile was there.

"I think we can let you stay."

Something in her chest ached, a sweet ache she didn't want to name just yet.

She dipped her head and breathed him in. He smelled of leather and pipe leaf and something deeper, earthy, and comforting. She filled her lungs, then stepped back and adjusted her skirts.

"Which one is yours?" she asked, her voice still soft beneath the scarf.

"I don't know," he said, mysterious as always.

She gave him a skeptical glance but followed him as he turned away from the pounding noise. Instead of heading deeper into the work zones, he cut across the yard toward a cinder block building in the center.

To her surprise, the noise faded as they approached. Flowerbeds lined the building, lush with color and motion. Bees hummed. The air was lighter here, touched with the sweetness of rosan and sun-warmed wood.

Rana knelt instinctively, her fingers brushing a vibrant bloom. She inhaled, and the city's stink vanished, chased away by floral perfume. She nearly picked it. Nearly tucked it behind her ear like she had as a child…

Then she felt eyes on her.

She looked up and saw Rhyslin standing on the wooden deck, watching her.

Guilt twisted in her chest, and she let go of the flower. Standing, she smoothed her skirts and adjusted the fall of her sword. She couldn't meet his gaze. *Why do I feel like a child caught sneaking sweets?*

She joined him silently, stealing a glance up at his face. No anger. No judgment. Just that calm, thoughtful expression. Her lungs loosened.

He opened the door, and they stepped into cool shadow. A narrow hallway led to a broader room filled with desks and drawing boards. The scent of oiled wood and ink tickled her nose. A herringbone floor guided them toward a display case filled with miniature ships.

As Rhyslin walked to the main desk and rang a small silver bell, Rana wandered to the display, eyes wide with curiosity. Each model was intricate and lovingly crafted. She traced a finger just above the glass, drawn in by the elegance of the ships.

Maybe one of these is ours, she thought.

Rana turned sharply at the deep, rumbling voice that called Rhyslin's name. The sound rolled through the flower-scented air like distant thunder.

Her eyes locked onto the man descending the staircase at the rear of the room, and her breath hitched.

He was massive, easily six and a half feet tall, with shoulders like a barn door and a chest broad enough to carry a horse. Blond hair, cropped short, gleamed under the overhead skylight, and jagged scars marked his tanned skin like battle-won trophies. One scar slashed cleanly through his right eyebrow, but his eye remained sharp and glinting with good humor. Another scar tugged at the corner of his mouth, yet it did little to hide the smile forming as he took in the room.

Rana blinked, wide-eyed. Her ears perked subtly under her scarf, and she instinctively stepped closer to Rhyslin.

"What bring you here? And who is this beautiful lass?" the giant asked, blue eyes sparkling as they settled on her.

"I'm here on business," Rhyslin deflected smoothly as the big man made to grab him in greeting. Sidestepping the bear-sized arms, he gestured toward her instead. "Jack, this is Rana, the daughter of one of my bannaichean."

That seemed to catch the man's attention properly. He paused mid-step and offered Rana a courteous half-bow. "It's a pleasure to meet ya, lass."

Rana dipped into a practiced curtsey, though her cheeks were warm behind the scarf. "An honor, Maighstir Mathan."

Jack Mathan chuckled heartily, then turned back to Rhyslin with a mischievous grin. "What woman in her right mind would bond wit' ye?"

Rhyslin raised a brow with mock offense. "Women with intelligence, grace, and impeccable taste, naturally."

"Women?" Jack's tone lifted in disbelief. "As in more than one?"

Rana fought to suppress her smile as Rhyslin solemnly nodded.

Jack let out a booming guffaw. "Next you'll tell me one o' them is that pale lass who sees the future."

"As a matter of fact," Rhyslin said coolly, "Rowena is my Treas bhann."

Mathan blinked in surprise and then looked genuinely impressed. "Well, I'll be damned." He leaned close, dropping his voice in mock conspiracy. "Why bond with the pale one, though?"

The draoidh shrugged. "Once I bonded with Flur and Ria, there was no reason to deny Rowena's request."

"Flur and Ria?" Mathan repeated, furrowing his brow. Then he tilted his chin toward Rana. "Wait, the lass's mother, right?"

"Yes," Rhyslin confirmed. "Ria is Rana's mother. A beautiful Hin i-daur of the burning sands. Long Auburn hair, warm brown eyes."

Mathan's laughter echoed again as he slapped his knee. "Then you had to bond with the pale one. That kind o' beauty makes a man brave, or stupid."

Rana stood silently beside Rhyslin, absorbing the exchange. She wasn't sure if Mathan meant it kindly, but the glimmer in his eye made her think he was testing Rhyslin's resolve more than questioning his judgment. She watched the two men, one lean, elegant, and sharp, the other large, brash, and warm, and realized something quietly affirming: Rhyslin belonged in every room, regardless of who filled it.

Rhyslin's jaw tightened as Jack Mathan's careless words hung in the air like smoke from a burning field. Disappointment curdled into disgust, and then that all-too-familiar cold rage settled across his shoulders like a wolf's mantle.

He raised his left hand slowly, deliberately, and pointed a single, accusatory finger at the shipwright. "I'll hear no more of you insulting my bannaichean."

Mathan blinked in surprise as Rhyslin stepped in, driving two fingers into the broad wall of muscle that was the man's chest. The jab had enough force to make even someone as solid as Mathan take a half-step back.

Rhyslin advanced, a storm behind his eyes. "If you can't show a measure of respect, I'll take my business elsewhere."

"Oy, there's no call for that!" Mathan blurted, his booming voice losing its typical jovial edge. The illusion of gold coins vanishing from his ledgers must have struck him harder than the poke. He lifted both hands in surrender, but Rhyslin wasn't done.

The anger still crackled under his skin, and he fought to keep it leashed. *This isn't like me. Is this the bonds? Or am I finally just tired of watching people mock what matters most to me?* The raw, possessive fury wasn't unfamiliar, but its intensity since bonding had grown. Ria would call it protective. Flur would call it justice. Rowena… might not call it anything at all.

Beside him, Rana stood poised, trying to appear unaffected. But the subtle tilt of her chin and the tightness in her shoulders gave her away. Rhyslin saw it all.

"Rhyslin?" Mathan asked, quieter now, the realization dawning like a cold sweat.

The draoidh turned his glare on him, voice low but sharp enough to draw blood. "Bear. Just shut up."

Mathan flinched at the old nickname. It landed like a verdict.

The room fell into uneasy silence. Mathan, once towering and loud, now seemed smaller somehow. Rhyslin gave him a moment, let him stew. Let him feel it. And when he finally spoke, his voice was cold steel.

"I don't know what your problem with Rowena is, but it ends now." He stepped closer, eyes narrowing. "You will show my bannan respect, or I will take my investments and walk. Do you understand?"

Mathan looked as if he'd taken a hammer to the chest. His shoulders slumped, and his ruddy face paled a shade. Rhyslin could see the conflict play out in real-time: the man wrestling between stubborn pride and the knowledge that losing the draoidh would be ruin.

He watched Mathan bow his head, eyes closed, lips moving silently in what looked like a prayer. *Good,* Rhyslin thought. *Let him sweat. Let him mean it.*

Out of the corner of his eye, he saw Rana watching with quiet intensity. Her expression had softened just slightly, no longer trying to feign detachment. Rhyslin gave her the smallest of nods before turning his attention fully back to Mathan, waiting for him to speak and to mean it.

Mathan bowed formally, the movement stiff but sincere, as he met Rhyslin's burning gaze. "I am sorry that I spoke ill of Miss Rowena," he said, his voice low and rough with regret.

When he dared to glance up, he saw the Draoidh's face, stone-edged, unreadable, but not entirely closed off.

That partial acceptance gave him just enough hope to speak again. He lifted his right hand to his chest, palm facing the sky, the old sign of honesty among the Brotherhood. "Rhyslin, if I may explain?"

Rhyslin's only reply was a subtle shift of his fingers on the staff, enough of a signal to proceed.

Mathan took a careful step forward, feeling the weight of the moment press into his chest. The faint scent of sawdust hung in the air, and the low hum of hammering from the yard beyond seemed a world away. He chose his next words with care.

"You always said you'd never bind yourself to a woman for life. Gods know you preached it like scripture."

He watched as Rhyslin's expression flickered, confirming that those words had been said and remembered. "So, when the pale lass came sniffing around, some of us thought... well, we thought she was looking for a comfortable nest."

The moment the words left his mouth, guilt curled in his gut like a fist. He saw the change in Rhyslin's posture, not anger, but sorrow. And something worse: disappointment.

Then came the whisper-soft reply. "Thank you for looking out for me."

Mathan blinked, unsure if he'd heard correctly.

Rhyslin's voice was steady but heavy with sadness. "You are ceangailte ann an gaol[8], are you not?"

Mathan's lips curved into a soft smile. His heart warmed despite the tension. "I am. With the blessings of Ananke and Chantico."

He gave his belly a playful slap. "D'ye think I got this way eating my own cookin'?"

A small huff of a laugh escaped Rhyslin, and Mathan seized the moment. "You never asked," he added, letting the grin settle in.

Rhyslin rubbed the back of his neck. "I feel like an asal."

"If it helps," Mathan said, voice rich with teasing sympathy, "you're not an asal all the time."

A long pause. Then Rhyslin sighed. "I suppose you're right."

Mathan raised an eyebrow. "You're just an old man set in his ways."

He expected a retort, but Rhyslin only nodded, his gaze dropping as if the truth had sunk in deep.

---

[8] Bound in love

Before Mathan could say more, Rhyslin straightened. He had the look of a man trying to move forward, and Mathan respected that.

"You didn't come here ta talk about the wee Mystic," Mathan said, letting his brogue roll freely now that the worst had passed. "You're here about yer cutter."

The Draoidh blinked, caught slightly off guard. Mathan grinned.

"It's doon," he said proudly, clapping his massive hands together. "Soon as ye bring a crew, she's yours to take home."

Rhyslin turned to glance at the girl, Rana, if he remembered correctly, who hid her expression beneath a scarf. Still, her eyes sparkled.

"That's good," Rhyslin replied. "I've enough of a crew to get her home."

Mathan chuckled deep in his chest. "Would ye like to see her?"

The glimmer in Rhyslin's eye was all the answer Mathan needed.

Rana marveled at the way joy softened Rhyslin's face, genuine, barely contained joy. Was it because the ship was ready? Or because he could finally leave this foul city behind?

A smile tugged at her lips at the thought of escaping Ause City's suffocating alley and returning home.

Her smile faded as a realization crept in like sunlight through the morning fog.

Did I just think of Am Flur Manse as home?

The thought rooted itself in her chest, firm and strange and warm. Yes. Yes, she had. It wasn't just a place. It was where she felt safe. Where she had begun to belong.

Her gaze shifted to Rhyslin, watching the way the light from above reflected the warmth in his smile.

She tilted her head, curiosity stirring deeper than she expected. -*What would it feel like if he were truly my father?* - The idea was ridiculous… wasn't it?

She was so lost in her thoughts that she didn't notice Rhyslin pass her, didn't hear the warmth in his voice when he said, "Come on, Rana." He was almost to the door before he paused, glancing over his shoulder.

"Rana?"

His voice finally reached her through the haze. She blinked, startled to find him watching her. "I'm sorry," she murmured. "I was… I got," Her words trailed off, caught in the throat of an emotion she didn't yet understand. Frustration burned behind her eyes. She hadn't felt this lost since her early days in *Comraich uisge na Gealaich.*[9]

Rhyslin's hand settled gently on her shoulder. Solid. Grounding. "Mathan and I are going to inspect the cutter," he said softly. "Would you like to join us?"

She shook her head, dark hair cascading like water across her back. Her eyes, those haunted, hazel depths, met his. The tears stung, unspilled, but he would see them anyway.

"Would it be alright if I stayed here?" she whispered. "Just for a little while?"

His eyes lingered on hers, understanding flickering there. He gave a quiet nod. "Of course," he said, giving her shoulder a reassuring pat. "I'll come get you when it's time to leave."

---

[9] Sanctuary of the Moonlit Waters

She watched him go, his footfalls fading toward the doorway. Her hands trembled slightly, so she folded them tightly into her lap and stared down at the intricate weave of the floor.

The moment the door clicked shut behind him, her composure shattered.

Rana curled forward in her seat, shoulders trembling as the tears broke free. Her whisper cracked the stillness like a splintering reed:

"Mathair… please help me. I don't want to feel like this anymore. I can't carry this pain."

No light shone through the window just yet, but she still hoped that somewhere, a goddess was listening.

CHAPTER TWELVE

The Dream of the Grove

In the stillness of the sacred glade, where time moved not in hours but in the slow breath of ancient trees, A' Mathair Astinmah made her gentle repose. Sunlight filtered through the high canopy of darach, oak thick with wisdom. It mingled with the dusky leaves of luaithre and the sharp, tangled limbs of dhroigheann, the blackthorn. A hush lay over the grove, broken only by the rustle of fern and the distant murmur of spring water. Sweet wildflowers spilled in joyful abandon around her bare feet, their fragrance perfuming the breeze with earthy joy.

The goddess tilted her head, a wreath of blossoms brushing her shoulders, her evergreen eyes narrowing slightly.

A whisper had ridden the wind, tremulous and desperate, a prayer stitched with sorrow and strength alike.

She bowed her head as the cry of a child found its way through the veil between realms. Not a child of blood, but of spirit. And the pain in the voice pierced her with tender ache.

Drawing a slow breath, she lifted one hand to the sky and loosed a melodic trill, soft and strange, like the music of river stones striking in rhythm.

Above her, branches stirred. The call was answered.

From the crown of the tallest darach, a pale-winged seabhag, a falcon as white as cloud foam, tipped in black, launched into the sky. Its wings beat like a priestess's prayer fan, parting the air with sacred intent.

It circled once, twice, then three times above the glade before descending in perfect grace to her extended wrist.

"How is my handsome sealgair today?" Astinmah murmured, brushing her fingers lovingly over the sleek plumage. The bird cocked its head, preening, intelligent eyes gleaming.

"You know, don't you?" she whispered. "You felt her too."

The falcon chirred softly.

"I want you to bring her to me." She raised her hand and painted Rana's tear-streaked face in a shimmer of light above her palm, fragile, proud, crumbling in solitude among wooden ships and memories. "The daughter of fire and dusk. She needs her mother now."

The seabhag gave a final call, a high, keening note that stirred the wildflowers and rang like crystal in the still air. With one beat of his wings, he launched upward. Light shimmered in his wake as he vanished into the Aether, the golden threads of his path unraveling behind him like a promise.

Astinmah lowered her hand and bowed her head once more, lips moving in silent benediction.

"Come home, mo ghaol[10]," she whispered. "Come where your heart will be known."

Rana had cried herself into a restless doze, her forehead resting against her arms at the drafting table. The dull ache in her chest pulsed with every shallow breath.

But when a damp breeze whispered across the back of her neck, she stirred with a soft whimper. The buzz of the construction yard was gone.

A symphony of birdsong replaced it, lilting and layered, descending like sunlight through trees. Her ears twitched. The air smelled different now; no dust or soot, only the fresh loam of a living forest and the sweet perfume of wildflowers and star-lilies.

She slowly lifted her head and blinked. The workshop was gone. In its place stood a forest glade of impossibly ancient trees, their branches twined high above like the vault of a green cathedral. Dappled light pooled on the mossy earth, and the hush of water reached her ears.

Rana rose cautiously, her fingers instinctively reaching for the hilt that should have been at her hip.

---

[10] My dear

Her heart pounded in her throat. Alone. Weaponless. The quiet pressed around her.

"Fear not, my child. You will not need your weapon here."

The voice, melodic and warm, came from behind. Rana turned, every muscle taut, and found a woman standing at the edge of the glade. She looked older than Rana's mother, with greying curls crowned by a living laurel of wildflowers. Wherever she stepped, the undergrowth parted, trees leaning to grant her passage. Her green eyes gleamed with ancient knowing.

Recognition bloomed in Rana's chest. She fell to her knees. "A Mhathair Astinmah, àlainn is dealrach, tiodhlaicear na beatha, banrìgh nan flùraichean[11]."

The goddess smiled, kneeling to gather Rana into a gentle embrace. The scent of spring honey and wild lilies clung to her. Rana melted into her warmth, feeling a sense of security and comfort, her eyes stinging, throat tight.

---

[11] Mother Astinmah. Bright, radiant, giver of life, queen of flowers.

Astinmah stroked her back. "What has brought such despair to a child of my trees?"

For a long moment, Rana couldn't speak. The Forest Mother's presence washed over her like a balm, easing the knots in her soul.

Her fingers curled in the goddess's robes. She was drowsy again, soothed by birdsong and the divine rhythm of the glade.

"How did I get here?" she whispered at last.

"You called to me," Astinmah said. "With your tears and your prayer, I heard you."

Rana pulled back slightly, confusion knitting her brow. "But... how can you not already know?"

The goddess gave a wistful smile. "Only He Who Watches sees all. I am the caretaker of what grows, not of what is hidden." Her gaze softened. "And we have met before, haven't we? At tri aibhnichean, then again at Am Flur Manse, and at the Talla na draoidheacd."

Rana nodded, voice hushed. "Yes, ma'am."

Astinmah tilted her head. "And yet you are surprised I remember you. Why?"

Rana bit her lip. "Because... I'm not special. Not like the others."

"Oh, little sapling." Astinmah cupped her face. "You are unique in ways you do not yet see."

Rana took a shuddering breath. "I've had the same dream for eight years. In it, I bond with Aon Socair. It's just the two of us. But now, Momma, Flur, and Rowena all share pieces of him. How can the bond I dreamed of still be real?"

Her voice cracked, and she turned her face into Astinmah's shoulder.

The glade held its breath as Astinmah's eyes sparked with dawning comprehension. Among the ancient darach trees and the curling boughs of luaithre and dhroigheann, the Forest Mother tilted her head, listening not just with her ears but with her spirit. Rana's desperate prayer had reached her, riding the wind like a fragile bird, and now Astinmah understood.

"Ah," she murmured, voice soft as rain over clover. "I think I understand."

She turned her gaze skyward, past the vaulted canopy and through the silver-spun veil of stars. Drawing herself up, she lifted her hand and summoned with divine clarity, "Anan-ke-inneal ceangail an anom. Despa leughadair ceò. I have need of you."

The constellations above shimmered, then slowly unraveled. A hush descended over the glade. Starlight fell like threads of silk as a rift split open in the sky. From the breach stepped two figures wrapped in power and presence.

The first, Ananke, was tall and stately, her hip-length brunette hair trailing behind her like river water, her white toga whispering with every step. Despoina followed, clad in a leather bustier over a cotan camisole, her skirt stitched with brass coins that sang a chiming rhythm with her every stride.

Both goddesses paused as they noticed the young woman nearby.

Despoina frowned, her voice sharp but laced with concern. "You used our soul names in front of the young one?"

Astinmah arched a brow, her smile cryptic. "Worry not, sister of the Fated Fog. She will not remember."

Despoina was not mollified, but she held her tongue and inclined her head. "What can we do for thee, Mathair Astinmah?"

"The child has dreamt for eight years of a bond she believes is unique," Astinmah said, shifting to the language of the diathan, her voice echoing like wind through pine. "But now she questions how that can be when others already share what she seeks."

The two goddesses exchanged a long glance, then turned their attention inward, gazes piercing time and fate. Astinmah remained silent, observing them with narrowed eyes.

Ananke spoke first, her voice calm and measured. "She has two bonds before her. One a lover's bond, the other a teaghlach bond." A familial bond.

Despoina followed more slowly, watching Rana's fate flicker in and out like candlelight in a breeze. "If she chooses the lover's bond, she will succeed in part. But the teaghlach bond... that one leads to fulfillment. To restoration. To home."

She hesitated. Astinmah noticed.

Something else stirred behind Despoina's gaze, a flicker of revelation she chose not to speak. Astinmah saw it and frowned but said nothing.

"I beg forgiveness, my mistress," Despoina said, folding her arms within her sleeves. "I am wearied. I must rest."

Astinmah inclined her head though suspicion tugged at her thoughts. *What do you withhold, sister?* But she did not ask. Some truths unfold only in time.

Ananke joined Despoina, the two vanishing through the shimmering portal. The glade quieted again.

Astinmah watched the fading light, then turned to Rana. The young woman stirred, confusion and vulnerability etched into every line of her form.

Leaning forward, Astinmah gently cupped Rana's face, her touch like mist over morning petals.

"Do not fear, mo leannan[12]," she whispered. "Your destiny remains. The bond you dream of is real. All you need do is reach for it."

She traced a rune across Rana's brow, her fingertip glowing faintly green.

"Sleep now. When you awaken, you will be back in your body. And when the time comes, you will remember only what your heart needs."

As Rana's breathing deepened into slumber, Astinmah exhaled and folded her hands, watching over the young daurwaith like a mother beside a cradle. The stars whispered above, and the glade resumed its quiet dreaming.

The scent of wildflowers was gone.

Rana stirred, her face still resting against the crook of her arm atop the drafting table. Her lashes fluttered as the world shifted sharply from soft birdsong to stillness, from sacred glade to varnished wood and iron-bound beams. The lighting felt dimmer here, heavier, more real.

A dull ache pressed behind her eyes. Her mouth was dry, her skin clammy with cooled tears. She sat up slowly, blinking at the scale models around her. The peace she'd felt in Astinmah's arms had vanished like a dream at sunrise.

And she was angry.

Fury tightened her chest, fast and sudden, until she could barely breathe. "It's not fair," she growled, her voice raw. Her fingers clenched into fists, nails digging crescents into her palms.

Her whole body thrummed with the need to move, to *do* something, anything. She eyed the model closest to her. It wouldn't take much to throw it. Not much at all.

Her hands twitched.

But then, she thought of him.

She closed her eyes and forced herself to breathe, slow and steady. One breath. Two.

She pictured Rhyslin.

The scent came first, beeswax and old parchment, the whisper of spell smoke lingering in the folds of his cloak. It filled her head, anchoring her. He was calm, always calm, even when danger struck. Even when that man had lunged at Momma, Rhyslin had only raised a single brow.

She wondered how he did it. Bitterness flowed like wild honey. How did he manage to carry so much and never falter?

Her heartbeat slowed. The tightness in her chest began to ease.

She looked again at the model. As satisfying as it might be to smash it, the image of Rhyslin's disappointment stopped her cold. Not his anger; no, she'd never truly seen him angry. But his disappointment? That quiet look, like he expected better of her, like he *believed* she could do better.

That would hurt more than any reprimand.

Her fists uncurled. She breathed out a shaky sigh and rubbed the lingering tear streaks from her cheeks.

Her gaze drifted to the sunlight slanting in through the high windows, dust motes swirling like tiny stars. Her thoughts, unbidden, wandered back to what she'd felt in the glade. The warmth. The longing. The ache.

Through her heart ache, she wondered again what it would like to be his daughter.

To be tethered not just by fate or prophecy but by *choice*. To be part of that strange, growing family, not just a guest or a student, but something more. Something *his*.

The idea both frightened and comforted her.

And in the stillness of that room, surrounded by silent ships and fading tears, Rana curled into herself and whispered to no one in particular:

"Someday, I'll be strong enough to ask."

CHAPTER THIRTEEN

The Cutter Made Ready

Rhyslin and Mathan approached the slip, their steps slowing as they neared the new cutter. The summer air was heavy with the scent of pine resin and sun-warmed tar; the sound of hammers and shouted orders from the yard carried on a low breeze. Nestled into the cradle of the dock, the new cutter's gleaming lines caught the sunlight, a testament to the craftsmanship that had gone into her creation.

"You painted the sheer strakes yellow?" Rhyslin asked, tilting his head. The golden stripe caught the light like the edge of a sun blade.

Mathan grinned. "If ye had house colors, we'd have matched 'em. Yer family's one of the oldest in the Saorsa, and ye've no personal colors?" He shook his head. "Shameful."

"Tell that to Flur and Ria," Rhyslin muttered with a chuckle. "I'm sure they're already working on it."

He moved closer, awe softening the lines of his face. His hand reached out, brushing along the curve of the hull. "My goodness, she's beautiful," he breathed. The hull looked poised to leap from her berth and dance on the wind. "You've outdone yourself, Bear."

Mathan puffed his chest with pride. "I've tried to make her more graceful. Look there," he pointed, "I've rounded her hull a bit. She won't buck the wind like some of your blocky war barges."

His words were a testament to his skill and attention to detail in the cutter's design.

Rhyslin crouched, inspecting the underside. "You flattened the keel. She'll be able to land without a docking frame?"

"Technically, aye," Mathan said, scratching his beard. "But I'd feel better if ye tested that part yerself."

"We can manage that," Rhyslin said, standing. "When's she ready to launch?" The anticipation of the upcoming voyage hung in the air, palpable and exciting.

Mathan's grin widened. "Soon as yer crew and passengers are aboard."

Rhyslin quirked a brow. "And elemental support?"

Mathan gave a knowing look. "I assumed ye brought the beautiful Ixa and the stalwart Andros with ye."

"I did." Rhyslin's smile faded into something more thoughtful. "They've been with Rembran ever since the tribunal. Ixa especially."

Mathan's brow furrowed. "Aye? She alright?"

Rhyslin hesitated. "As well as can be. She was abused by a mage I'd trusted. Ixa's healing, but... slowly."

The shipwright's voice dropped, heavy with sympathy. "Poor dear. Night terrors?"

"And tremors. But the magaidh's been dealt with." Not the entire truth, but close enough. Nobody outside the Talia knew Meron had turned traitor. "Rana and Rembran were ready to kill him if he looked at her sideways."

"Rana? That Rana? The one sittin' in my office like a summer breeze?"

Rhyslin's voice held a note of pride. "The very same. She and Ixa are thick as thieves."

Mathan blinked. He'd seen the girl's slim build, the way she moved, more grace than threat. "Ye think she could do it? Kill a man?"

Rhyslin didn't hesitate. "Without blinking. She's nearly bested Rembran. Took Marcus to a draw. Would've beaten him outright if he hadn't used his old ranger magic."

Mathan winced at the memory of that trick, vines snaking up from the earth. "Has she beaten anyone, then?"

A slow grin spread across Rhyslin's face. "Let me tell you about the day she fought Lieutenant Sparhawk."

As the draoidh spoke, painting the scene in the council chamber, the shattering of the crystal, the shocked silence, and Sparhawk's bloodied face, Mathan found himself listening in stunned silence.

When Rhyslin finished, Mathan gave a low whistle. "I've seen the lad. Big fella. Didn't think she had it in her."

"Most don't, until it's too late," Rhyslin said. "Rana doesn't just fight. She thinks. She adapts."

Mathan looked back toward the office, sobered. "I'll not make her angry, then."

"Wise," Rhyslin chuckled. Then his eyes returned to the cutter. "What about this mystery crew you mentioned?"

Mathan's mood shifted as he folded his arms. "Ye remember that freak storm a few weeks back?"

"How could I forget? Astinmah summoned it herself."

"It shook the winds as far as Spiorad Dorcha: two brigs and a transport caught in it. One brig and that transport limped in here after. Yer temporary crew is from the Gryphon."

Rhyslin nodded slowly, absorbing that. He stepped closer to the cutter and laid a hand on her polished flank. The timber was warm beneath his palm. "She's ready to fly, then?"

"Aye," Mathan said with satisfaction. "Jes' as soon as ye give the word."

Rhyslin exhaled a long, measured breath, the stink of the city left behind him for the first time in days. He could already feel the pull of open skies.

"Then all we wait for is Sparhawk's squad."

Mathan clapped him on the shoulder. "Sooner ye leave this cursed city, the better. I see it in yer eyes."

Rhyslin didn't answer, but his eyes remained on the sky, already measuring the wind.

Rana fought to regain control of her turbulent emotions just as the door creaked open. The sudden burst of sound, clanging metal, shouting workers, and the sharp tang of resin and cut wood shattered the heavy silence like a thrown stone. Rhyslin entered with Mathan behind him, and the door swung shut once more, muffling the chaos outside.

She stiffened, guilt rising hot under her collar. Her head jerked up, her eyes colliding with Rhyslin's steady gaze.

He didn't say a word, but his eyes flicked over her flushed cheeks, and her clenched hands, then scanned the room, brow arched in mild curiosity. Nothing looked out of place, but she felt it all the same. Seen. Exposed.

Rana dropped her gaze, teeth catching on her lower lip. She didn't speak. Couldn't, not with Mathan still in the room.

A few exchanged words later, the shipwright vanished into his office.

"Do you want to talk about it?" Rhyslin's voice was low, gentle. Not demanding, inviting.

He crossed the room in two strides and extended his right hand.

Rana stared at it, her pulse a nervous flutter in her ears. She didn't trust herself to speak. She simply nodded and bowed her head, eyes burning.

Why do I feel like this? Why does looking at him make me ache and want to run at the same time?

When her trembling fingers brushed his palm, he didn't hesitate. He drew her into his arms with the same quiet strength he always carried. Her face found the curve of his shoulder, the scent of beeswax, old parchment, and fresh cut holly wrapping around her like a blanket.

She buried her head against his chest and fought the sob, clawing its way up her throat.

Rana trembled in his arms, and Rhyslin tightened his embrace, gently brushing his thumb along her back.

"It's okay, *mo phrìseil*," he whispered, his voice low and steady in her ear. "If you can hold on just a moment longer, we'll find a quiet place. Just us."

He felt her nod against his chest, a subtle shift that sent a pang through his heart. She was holding on by threads. He closed his eyes, steadied his breathing, and reached outward. *[Marcus.]*

Marcus hadn't moved an inch.

From a distance, he looked asleep, hat tipped low over his face, boots crossed at the ankle, shoulder resting lazily against the warm stone wall of the construction yard. Nat curled into his side like a red-haired shadow, breathing soft and slow. But Marcus was anything but asleep.

He noted the sound of Ixa's quiet sigh, the faint grind of pebbles falling from Andros' hand. Even the way Rembran subtly shifted his weight, ever protective. A grain of sand drifted from Andros' palm to Marcus' boot. He didn't flinch.

Then it came.

A sharp prickle danced down his spine. He blinked once, slowly. Not Nat. This had weight.

Another jab, more insistent. Marcus sighed inwardly.

[What do ya want, Rhys?]

[I forgot how hard it is to communicate this way.]

A low smirk tugged at Marcus' lips. *[Mind stones are easier, old man.]*

[Mine's at the manor.] Rhyslin didn't bother hiding his annoyance. *[If you're done laughing, I need a favor.]*

The humor slipped from Marcus' expression. He straightened slightly, just enough to hear better.

[Go on.]

[Send Rembran and his shadows in. The cutter is ready.]

Marcus let out a short whistle. Rembran looked up from where he stood, caught the signal, and nodded once. The spell-blade turned and murmured something to Ixa and Andros. All three disappeared through the gate without another word.

[Done. Anything else?]

Rhyslin hesitated. Rana was still trembling faintly, her breathing short, shallow.

[Yes. Check on my bannaichean. Then meet us in the field near the council chamber. One hour.]

Marcus smiled again. Finally, the air was already feeling lighter. *[Gladly. We'll see you there.]*

Back inside, Rhyslin gently nudged Rana just enough to look into her eyes. She refused to meet his gaze, cheeks flushed and eyes still glassy.

But she was standing. She hadn't broken.

And for now, that was enough.

Rhyslin closed his eyes and reached inward, brushing the delicate golden thread of his bond with Flur.

He found her and felt her yearning pulse across the distance like a flickering candle, but no words followed. There was only the echo of her presence, pressed against a barrier too thick to break. A dull ache tugged at his chest as her frustration shimmered faintly through the link, the emotional equivalent of clenched fists and unshed tears.

He tried to reach deeper, but before he could, another bond stirred, warm, rich, and steady as hearth fire.

{Flur's frustrated, mo graidh,} Ria's voice slipped into his mind, soft as silk and threaded with concern. *{She wants so badly to speak across the distance.}*

A slow breath escaped him, grounding him. He leaned one shoulder against a nearby beam, the scent of aged wood and sawdust lingering in the air, earthy and real.

{*What did you need?*}

He smiled slightly, touched as always by how effortlessly Ria could reach him, how instinctively she soothed, even across a city.

{*For you, Flur, and Rowena to gather what you can. Marcus is on his way to escort you to the cutter.*}

{*It's about time,*} she replied, her relief unmistakable. {*How much can we bring?*}

{*Only what you can carry,*} he warned. {*There won't be much time to unload cargo before we leave the manse and head straight to San Ang's.*}

A playful flicker curled through the bond.

{*We won't forget the iced cream.*}

That earned a real smile. His eyes crinkled at the corners.

[*As if you would.*]

There was a gentle pause, no words, just warmth, and then:

{*We'll see you soon, mo ghraidh.*}

Her voice faded like the last note of a lullaby, leaving him with the faint echo of her calm.

Rana curled deeper into the soft corner of the couch, the quiet hush of the office sheltering her from the clamor of the shipyard beyond the door. Her hands trembled faintly, tucked against her sides, and her eyes, red-rimmed and heavy, fixed on the low-burning lantern above Rhyslin's desk. It reminded her of home. Or... what she was starting to think of as home.

Rhyslin's voice cut through the quiet, low, and gentle. "Do you still want to talk about it?"

She could only nod, her throat tight. He led her to a simple wooden door, the one she hadn't dared to approach earlier. When he opened it with a flick of his fingers and a half-smile, he said, "Step into my office."

The moment she stepped inside, Rana froze. This wasn't just an office. It was nearly identical to his study at Am Flur Manse. The leather chair near the hearth. The faint herbal scent of elder wood and beeswax polish. Even the sound of floorboards under her boots had the same resonance. Her eyes darted to his in surprise.

He nodded, confirming what her senses had already told her, and she crossed the room, skirts whispering around her ankles, before sinking onto the far end of the couch.

Rhyslin closed the door behind them and crossed the room. She shifted, instinctively creating distance, retreating into the corner. His brow creased slightly, but he didn't push.

"What's wrong, mo phrìseil?"

The nickname broke her. Her breath hitched, and before she could stop herself, her face was buried in her palms, hot tears seeping through her fingers.

"I prayed to A' Mathair," she choked out between sobs. Her voice trembled as she painted the memory, the glade, the songbird, the goddess. Astinmah's arms around her. Her scent, star-lilies and loam. Then Ananke. Then Despoina. Their answers and their silences.

"She said the bonds are still there. That my path is still open if I want it," Rana whispered. "But then she just sent me back, like none of it mattered. No warning. No clarity. Nothing."

She wiped her cheeks, furious at herself. "I almost destroyed one of the model ships. I was so angry." Her voice cracked again. "Are you disappointed in me?"

She kept her eyes closed, unable to face the answer.

"No," Rhyslin said quietly. "Did you destroy it?"

She shook her head.

"Then I'm proud of you for not giving in to that anger."

She opened her eyes slowly. His arms were open.

Rana hesitated a heartbeat, then crawled into his lap, curling against his chest. His warmth sank into her, soothing her frayed nerves. His fingers moved gently down her back, slow and grounding.

"You're not the first person to wrestle with A' Mathair's mysteries," he murmured into her hair.

"How do you always stay so calm?" she asked, her voice barely audible.

"I've had years of practice," he answered, brushing his lips against the tip of her right ear.

A shiver fluttered through her. She leaned back, looking into his eyes. They held no judgment, only warmth. Love. Steady and unwavering.

"Why couldn't you have been my father?" she asked softly. The question surprised even her.

She reached up and cupped his cheek. When he wiped a tear from her jaw, she leaned into his palm like a flower tilting toward the sun.

"I could always adopt you," he said.

The offer struck like thunder. Her breath caught. "Do you mean it?"

"If you want it, I can make it happen."

A hundred emotions clawed through her. Joy. Terror. Hope. Confusion. She wanted to say yes and yet feared what it would mean. The part of her that longed for a father warred with the part that dreamed of something more.

"May I think about it?" she whispered.

Rhyslin nodded. "Take all the time you need."

She tried to smile. "Do we have to go back out there?"

"Not until the cutter is ready."

Relief eased into her bones, and she leaned into him again. Time slowed. His heartbeat became the metronome of her world, each steady thump reassuring her that she was safe. Her thoughts grew hazy.

Why do I always feel like sleeping in his arms? Is it his prana? Or because I feel so safe?

She shifted slightly, nestling against him, and for a moment, instinct and longing, pulled her fingers toward his hand. She paused. Breathed. And chose stillness instead.

When the knock came, it was too soon.

Rhyslin didn't move. "Yes?"

"Sir? Captain Rembran sends his regards. The ship is ready to lift."

She exhaled and slid out of his lap, fixing her skirt. "Every time," she muttered.

As he moved to the door, she stopped him and held out her scarf.

"Help me?"

He took it, his fingers deft and warm as he wrapped it around her ears without catching her hair.

When he opened the door, she followed, falling into step beside him. And for the first time in hours, her chest didn't feel quite so tight.

CHAPTER FOURTEEN

The Cutter and the Cloud Maiden

The *Cloud-Dancer* was smaller than the *Dawn-Breaker* by leagues. Still, Rhyslin found the deck beneath his boots steadier than he expected, eager, almost as if the cutter itself was waiting to fly. The wind off the harbor carried salt and sun-warmed tar, curling through the taut rigging and humming low through the hull. His duster whispered against his legs as he crossed the deck, boots thudding softly on the planks. Behind him, Rana followed, light-footed but alert, her ever-twitching ears tuned to something more than sound.

The quarterdeck rose ahead, just a few steps, nothing grand, but tradition still held. Rhyslin paused before stepping up, letting his presence settle like a weight against the tension in the air.

Cutters didn't need a wheel, too small, too lean for pomp, just a tiller, simple and honest. And the man manning it was right where he should be.

Rembran glanced up from his quiet conversation and offered a sloppy, two-fingered salute.

"Welcome aboard, sir."

Rhyslin raised a brow, unimpressed.

"I know I taught you better than that, *Captain*."

There was an edge to his voice, not anger, but the kind of disappointment that could still cut deeper. He held Rembran's gaze.

The spell-blade shifted his stance, his expression tightening. He brought his fist to his chest, then extended it palm-up toward Rhyslin in the proper Saor-Shelbh salute. His voice, when it came, held both precision and pride.

"Welcome aboard the cutter *Cloud-Dancer*, sir."

He didn't drop the salute until Rhyslin returned it, crisp and measured. Power might shift aboard ships, but respect never did.

Rhyslin's eyes drifted to the tiller and the man guiding it with the casual grace of someone who had nothing left to prove.

"Andros," he said, the corner of his mouth lifting. "Have you become a helmsman now?"

The elemental turned, still in his plainsman's form, dark braid down his back, sun-dark skin, steady hands. One rested lightly on the tiller as if it had grown from his palm.

"I may have," Andros replied with a faint smile. "This tiller makes the cutter more responsive than your galleon."

Rhyslin threw back his head and laughed, warm and unrestrained.

"The galleon's a beast. She turns like a tired ox. This little one," he gestured with a sweep of his coat, "looks like she was born for mischief."

He scanned the deck briefly, reading it like a battle map, tight crew, good posture, minor scuffs on the mainsheet cleat, then turned back to Andros.

"Where's Ixa?"

"Below," Andros said, nodding toward the aft hatch. "Helping the loadmaster balance the cargo."

Rhyslin nodded, more relieved than he let show. "Of course she is. Tireless as ever."

He turned back to Rembran. "Are we ready to lift ship, Captain?"

Rembran took a breath, cast a sharp glance around the deck, then nodded once.

"We are sir."

"Then lift ship," Rhyslin said, turning on his heel. "We've waited long enough."

As he walked away, the ship seemed to exhale beneath him. He felt it, a subtle shift in the grain of the wood, a gentle hum in the soles of his boots. Not just readiness. Eagerness.

The elementals were stirring.

He caught Rana's footsteps just behind his own and the quiet swish of her coat. She hadn't spoken once since they boarded, but he could feel her gaze on him. Not assessing. Just...watching. Listening.

Good.

Let her see.

Rhyslin didn't look back, but the wind caught the edges of his coat and flared it like a banner behind him.

This was his ship now.

And soon, the sky would be too.

Rembran watched Rhyslin vanish below deck, boots echoing on the narrow steps. The spell-blade-turned captain let out a breath through his nose, half focus, half nerves, and rolled his shoulders like a man about to wrestle something twice his size.

He turned to face the deck. The wind tugged at the rigging with growing insistence, and the cutter creaked, impatient for the sky.

"All stations, prepare for lift!" he barked. "Release clamps! Secure all lines! Tiller to ready!"

A flurry of motion followed, boots striking planks, hands hauling line, shouts echoing across the hull like heartbeat and breath. A sharp **clang** rang out as the final dock clamp disengaged. The *Cloud-Dancer* shifted underfoot, free.

Before Rembran could call the lift, a rush of energy crackled behind him.

Ixa came flying up from below deck, auburn hair a storm about her face. Her eyes scanned the deck, wild and alert, until they found him. She crossed to him quickly, still barefoot from working below.

"Are we lifting?" she asked, her voice light but tinged with strain.

"Aye." Rembran nodded. "Rhyslin wants us airborne. Balance it on the way if you can."

Ixa frowned and ran a hand through her hair, pushing strands behind one ear. The wind lifted them again almost immediately.

"She's new, mo ghraidh. Not fully loaded. The designers *think* they know how she'll fly, but I don't trust guesswork." She leaned close, fingers brushing his arm. Her voice dropped. "Neither should you."

He met her sky-blue eyes and saw more than magic there, concern, love, trust earned in shadow and fire.

"Just do your best," he murmured, thumb brushing her wrist. "At least this run's short."

A voice floated over from the tiller.

"Oh? And where are we going?" Andros asked, his eyes never leaving the horizon.

Rembran lifted his chin. "To the landing field near the council hall, I imagine. Somewhere flat enough to bury a mistake."

Andros gave a minute nod, and Ixa moved to stand at Rembran's side. He took a long breath, scanned his crew, steady at their posts, waiting on him, and then whispered low.

"Get us above the treetops."

"Yes, mo ghraidh," Ixa murmured.

She stepped to the portside rail and pressed her palm to the wood. It thrummed under her fingers like something breathing. Her magic whispered down into the keel, rising through the grain, spreading outward.

<Lighter than air. Lift. Balance. Rise.> The Cloud-Dancer answered.

With a low moan of timber and a flex beneath their feet, the cutter began to ascend. Sails angled automatically as the crew trimmed lines; the wind caught and filled them with a thunderclap of fabric. The ship trembled. The air tasted of ozone and lifted hairs at the nape like a coming storm.

Ixa staggered. Her knees buckled, and she pitched forward into Rembran's waiting arms. Her skin had gone paper-pale, and her breath came shallow.
A curl of mist trailed from her shoulders, invisible to most, but thick with effort spent.

"Ixa,"

"I'm fine," she lied. "But the balance, this hull wasn't trimmed. We're skewed to starboard. It's pulling everything sideways. I can't hold it,"

A sudden vibration rolled through the deck, a heartbeat of resonance like something old had awakened.

It echoed not just in the hull but in bone and blood, the ship remembering what it was made to do.

Rhyslin emerged at the top of the stairs, eyes sweeping the quarterdeck. He crossed in three strides, already reading the situation. The wind stilled around him, pausing in deference.

"Ixa?" he said, sharp.

She tried to stand, peeling away from Rembran's support, but the effort trembled through her limbs. The deck itself seemed to lean slightly, as if undecided whether to help or collapse.

"The balance isn't right," she confessed. "It's taking all my strength to keep her from capsizing mid-air."

Rhyslin's brow furrowed, then cleared. He reached for the staff strapped across his back and held it out without ceremony. "Take it."

She stared at it. "Rhyslin,"

"Take it."

Her fingers closed around the staff.

The moment her skin touched the carved surface, it sang.

Not with words, not with melody, but with memory and magic. Wind, sky, pressure, purpose. It resonated along her bones like thunder chasing lightning. Her knees straightened. Her lungs filled.
The air around her calmed, as if drawn inward to listen.

"It's singing," she breathed, eyes wide. "It's alive."

Rhyslin nodded, his voice softer now. "He was made to channel the sky. He likes you."

The ship leveled, steady now, no more fighting against her own bones. The deck settled like a held breath released. A faint shimmer of light passed along the railing, like the vessel exhaled relief.

Rhyslin turned to Rembran, his tone shifting back to command.
"When we land and load Sparhawk's supplies," he said, "take as many men as you need and balance the cargo properly."

Rembran lowered his eyes. "Aye, sir."

"Tch." Rhyslin clicked his tongue and shook a finger. "You made a mistake, captain. But it's only a failure if you don't learn from it."

He clapped Rembran on the shoulder with a touch of warmth. "Everyone slips. If you don't believe me, ask O'Cuire about the cask of Agus dearg that cracked open because he forgot to check the spirit rack."

Rembran groaned. "Gods save me. I remember that smell."

Ixa laughed softly beside him, still holding the staff, her color returning slowly.
The wind teased her hair, gentle now, as if in apology.

Rhyslin smiled just enough for the wind to catch the edges of it. A dry breeze curled past his collar, warm as praise.

"Let's not add any new legends today," he said. "Get us to the council field in one piece."

The cutter glided low over the tree line, sails slackening as the wind died around the council grounds. From his place at the tiller, Andros scanned the wide stone field ahead, polished pale and glowing in the afternoon sun. Stone arches flanked the council hall's high steps, banners barely stirring in the stillness.

"We're almost there," he called out, adjusting the trim. "How close to the council hall do you want to be?"

Rhyslin, leaning on the quarterdeck rail, gave him a crooked smile. "As close as you can. No reason for them to haul gear across a field just to meet us."

Andros grunted, a low sound of agreement. "Ah, there's a slip near the door. Tight fit, but I'll set her down there."

The air shifted. Ropes groaned in their pulleys as the cutter dipped into its descent. Below deck, barrels creaked. A faint shimmer of draoidheacd trailed in their wake like dust disturbed. The world held still, as if watching.

The keel touched down with a firm bump, just enough to jar knees and rattle teeth. The cutter swayed once, then stilled.

On the quarterdeck, Rembran barely noticed the landing. His eyes were fixed on Ixa, who slumped at the rail, still seated where Rhyslin had left her. Her skin looked pale beneath her auburn hair, and faint sparks shimmered around her fingertips, magic still seeping out of her like air from a cracked flask.

He didn't move.

"You gonna stand there all day or balance the stowage?" Rhyslin's voice cut through the quiet.

When Rembran didn't respond, Rhyslin stepped over and gave him a firm shove.
"Move it, captain. You've got a job to do."

Rembran turned slowly, eyes flashing. There was no anger in them, just shame.

"I'll take care of Ixa," Rhyslin said, calm as morning frost.
A cold clarity settled over the deck in his wake.

Rembran swallowed whatever he wanted to say and stalked off, barking orders as he went. "All hands below! Balance the gods-damned load before she lifts crooked again!"

Rhyslin waited until the last of the crew vanished down the ladder before crouching beside Ixa.

The auburn-haired Elemental gave him a dazzling smile, right before she passed out, and would have hit the deck. Before she could, Rhyslin caught her. "Ixa."

She didn't answer, couldn't. Even the smell of rain and clouds was fading away. That loss hit like silence after song.

"Ixa?"

When she still did not answer, he gathered her to him, scooping her up in his arms. With a grunt, Rhyslin started down the stairs that led to the main deck. At the bottom of the stairs, he started down the main deck, heading to the gangplank. Every board beneath his boots felt aware of her weight, his urgency.

As he passed Rana, her desert rose scent cracked as she saw Ixa. "Maighstir." She couldn't say anything else, as Rhyslin interrupted her.

"Go get my staff and meet me in the council hall." His order sharp, backed up by the smell of iron and steel.

It so startled Rana that she took off down the deck, running as if death hounds were nipping at her heels.

With Rana dispatched and, on her way, Rhyslin achieved his goal and started down the gangplank.
The air thinned beneath him, tension coiled in every step.

Halfway down, he was forced to stop when Sparhawk barred his way, one crate of supplies on his shoulder. The scout leader quickly stepped to one side, balancing himself on the edge of the plank. "Do you need help with her, old man?" His respectful humor bolstered by the smell of wood and packing materials.

Rhyslin shook his head, "No. I've got her. But thank you for asking, Lieutenant." He slightly shifted Ixa's weight and continued down the gangplank.

As he set foot on the ground, the grass cushioned his steps, adding just enough of a spring to propel him on the way to the council hall.

The earth itself bore them gently, as if recognizing one carried light and one carried storm.

With the information Rhyslin gave her, it didn't take long for Rana to find the staff.

Her boots clattered softly on the deck as she sprinted up to the quarter deck, skirts fluttering behind her like dark silk banners. The sun was falling, casting warm gold light across the planks and setting the rigging aglow. The cutter creaked softly beneath her feet, settling after the flight, the scent of sun-warmed wood, sea salt, and faint elemental residue still hanging in the air.

There it was.

Exactly where Rhyslin said it would be, leaning against the rail, six feet of polished black wood. Silver runes etched into its surface shimmered faintly, pulsing with life just below sight. A slow smile curled across her lips as she reached out and closed her fingers around the staff.

Warm. Strangely warm. And humming.

Rana froze.

The moment her skin touched it, the world narrowed. Sound bloomed.

It started as a single tone, clear, crystalline, vibrating behind her sternum like the first pluck of a harp string. Then came more: a harmony that rose in slow, deliberate layers. Flutes wove through it like wind in leaves. Drums pounded low and ancient as if the heartbeat of the earth itself had been captured in song.

Then came the voices.

They weren't words exactly but *truths*, sung rather than spoken, as if the staff carried not only language, but memory. Images spilled across her mind in sweeping rhythm: stars born in silent fire, roots pushing through newborn soil, the first breath of life shivering through ancient forests. The world, the whole of *Crann Na Beatha*, unfolded before her like a tapestry drawn in song.

She didn't breathe. Couldn't.

Her ears twitched, attuned not to sound but to *feeling*. A pulse of joy moved through her limbs. The ache in her body, the lingering fatigue from training, the self-doubt she rarely voiced, was soothed, melted away like frost beneath spring light.

Peace, her soul whispered. *This is what it was meant to feel like.*

And then…

The music shifted.

One final chord, drawn out too long. It soured slightly at the edge. An ominous undertone surfaced, dissonant and cold, like a shadow behind silk. Then silence.

It cut off mid-phrase, leaving her gasping in the void it left behind.

Rana blinked, disoriented, blinking against the light as the wind stirred her hair. The staff no longer sang. It no longer hummed. It was just wood again.

She stared down at it, silver runes winking in the sunlight as if it had never done anything at all.

"Why did you stop singing?" she whispered, pulling it close to her chest. It was still warm and comforting but now stubbornly quiet. She tilted her head, watching it like one might a moody cat.

Raising an eyebrow, she exhaled slowly. "Oh, come on," she muttered.

The antechamber was cool and dimly lit, its polished stone floor whispering beneath Rhyslin's boots. Faint golden light filtered through high, narrow windows, catching dust motes that hung suspended like stars. The air held the scent of parchment, and the lingering magic of old spells long settled into the walls.

The moment he stepped inside, his bhannan moved toward him, quick, concerned steps echoing softly in the stillness. But they halted as one when they saw what he carried.

Ixa.

Slumped in his arms, her auburn hair trailing like burnt silk over his shoulder, her limbs unmoving.

It was Ria who caught herself first. She reached out and gently stopped Flur and Rowena with a hand at their arms. Her voice was low and steady.

"What happened?"

Rhyslin crossed to one of the benches by the far wall and laid Ixa down with great care. Her body felt too light. Too quiet.

"She overextended," he said, brushing a lock of hair from Ixa's cheek. "She kept the *Cloud-Dancer* in the air, despite the stowage imbalance. Held her steady through the entire flight."

He paused, frowning as he looked at her still form.

"And I think she burned herself out doing it."

Flur stepped forward, her brows furrowed in concern. Her skirts whispered as she knelt beside Ixa and reached out with a careful hand. Her fingertips brushed the elemental's brow and instantly stilled.

"She feels — empty," she whispered. The word felt wrong in her mouth. Too final. Too cold.

Rhyslin didn't respond. His eyes were closed, hands hovering above Ixa's form as he reached inward with his senses.

"Mo ghraidh?" Flur prompted gently. "Are you listening?"

"Hmm?" He opened one eye, caught the tight frown between her brows, and exhaled. "I'm sorry. No, I wasn't. Something's wrong. I can't find her energy. It's like —"

He trailed off, brow tightening.

Flur studied him for a beat longer. Then, her features softened. She reached out and took his hand.

"Come," she said, guiding his fingers to Ixa's forehead. "Here. Let me show you."

Rhyslin followed her lead, letting his senses settle. And this time, he felt it.

Or rather, the *absence* of it.

The elemental pathways that should have shimmered through Ixa's being, like silver threads of starlight, were instead dull. Dim. Like embers that had burned out but still held their shape.

"That's not good," he muttered.

Flur's eyes fluttered shut, and she whispered a prayer to Mathair, drawing on her own gentle grace.

"Please," she breathed. "Let me see what he sees."

In her mind's eye, the map of Ixa's body unfolded, veins and arteries threaded with energy. Only instead of bright coursing mana, what she saw were near-black channels, like dried riverbeds.

Her eyes opened wide and fearful.

"Why is it so dark?"

"Why indeed?" Rhyslin echoed, more to himself than to her. He sat back with a sigh. "I think she nearly drained her mana reserves."

Flur tilted her head slightly. "Mana?" The word scratched at something familiar. "Is that — bad?"

"Yes," he replied, shifting into a posture she recognized: lecture mode. "Very. You see, elementals like Ixa and Andros aren't like us. In their home planes, they are *pure*, air, water, fire, earth. When summoned, they take shape based on the image or expectations of the summoner."

Flur blinked, thinking it through.

"So — they didn't *look* like this before?"

"No," he said, glancing at Ixa. "We can thank Rembran's imagination for their current forms."

Flur giggled through her concern. She could picture Rembran's taste perfectly. But her smile faded as another question bloomed.

"How are they different from us?" she asked, more softly now. Her gaze drifted back to Ixa.

Rhyslin shifted slightly, leaning forward, elbows resting on his knees. His voice dropped to something quieter.

"Our lives are bound to spirit. We grow older, our prana thins, and when it's gone, we return to the Wheel. But elementals — they're tied to mana. Ambient draoidheacd keeps them grounded here."

Flur listened, breath held. She could feel the turn in his voice, how the words pressed against something deeper.

"And you?" she asked gently. "And Marcus?"

Rhyslin looked at her. There was silence in his expression, one weighted with centuries.

"Marcus," he said finally, "will live so long as his curse holds. Forever, unless something breaks him."

She moved closer, laying her hands on his shoulders.

"And you?"

Rhyslin inhaled. The bench creaked softly under his shifting weight.

"So long as there is draoidheacd in this world," he said, voice quiet and unwavering, "I believe I will never die."

For a heartbeat, Flur just looked at him. Then she leaned forward and pressed her lips to his.

It was gentle. Intimate. A kiss filled with the weight of forever and the fragility of the present.

When she pulled back, her eyes shimmered.

"I will love you to the end of my days," she whispered. "And I will fill our house with joy, love, and peace."

He started to speak, but she pressed a finger against his lips.

"Later," she smiled, knowing his thoughts. "I promise."

Then she looked back at Ixa, her voice sobering again.

"If we're tied to prana — what do they use?"

Rhyslin blinked, shaking himself back to focus.

"Mana. They draw on ambient energy to remain anchored here. But it burns quickly. They must return to their home planes, *Tir Nan Neoil,* in Ixa's case, to refill their reserves."

"How often?" Flur asked, brows furrowed.

"It varies," he said. "But usually, every two or three days."

She exhaled, already knowing the answer to her next question.

"Has she returned home since she bonded with Rembran?"

"I don't know," he admitted.

Flur's expression turned resolute. "Then we ask him."

Rhyslin nodded. "Agreed. But until then, she needs to go home. She won't recover here."

He looked toward the archway leading out of the antechamber.

"I'll need my staff to open a gate," he murmured. "Rana should be bringing it soon."

The moment Rhyslin whispered of needing his staff, the doorway cracked open and **Rana** slipped through like a wisp of wind.

Her cheeks were flushed from running, and her hazel eyes sparkled when they found him kneeling beside Ixa's still form.

"Here's your staff, *Maighstir*," she said, breathless but beaming, as she stepped forward and extended it with both hands. "Momma, you won't believe what happened. The staff," she paused, her voice reverent now, "it *sang* to me."

Silence rippled through the chamber.

Every head turned toward her, stunned. Even **Flur**, who had seen many strange wonders, blinked.

Rhyslin, however, simply inclined his head, his face unreadable. As though someone had told him the sea was wet.

He took the staff with care. It was still warm from Rana's grip, its silver runes faintly aglow, like embers beneath the ash.

Without another word, he turned back to Ixa. His brows furrowed in focus, and the staff hummed in response as he called upon its power.

Light gathered at its tip, drawn inward, then stretched outward as if tugging on unseen threads. Ixa's body shimmered, her edges softened, limbs beginning to blur into mist.

For one aching heartbeat, it worked.

Then everything went wrong.

The glow fractured. A pulse of raw energy cracked through the room like ice breaking underfoot.

Ixa gasped, pain seizing her face. Her body snapped back into solidity, her back arching in unconscious protest before collapsing again. Her skin had gone even paler. Damp.

Rhyslin inhaled sharply. "I was afraid of that," he murmured.

Behind him, someone moved.

No, *charged.*

Boots thundered against the floor outside, accompanied by hoarse shouting:

"Make space!"

"Move, get out of the bloody way!"

"Stand clear!"

The door slammed open, and Rembran burst through, sweat on his brow, his chest heaving as if he'd sprinted a mile.

"What did you do, Rhyslin?" he demanded, clutching at his chest. "It felt like, like my heart was about to explode."

Rhyslin stood slowly. "I tried to send her back to *Tir Nan Neoil,*" he said quietly.

Rembran turned toward the bench, and when his eyes landed on Ixa, his heart seemed to stop again. She looked so small. So still. Her skin was nearly translucent.

"Why is she still here?" he choked out.

"I can't release her," Rhyslin admitted. "Something's anchoring her."

Rembran's face twisted, fear, frustration, guilt.

"What do I do?" His voice cracked. "Rhyslin, what do I do? I don't want to lose her."

Rhyslin placed a steady hand on the younger man's shoulder.

"Tell her she can go home."

Rembran flinched.

"If your bond is true," Rhyslin said gently, "she'll come back. But she needs your permission to leave."

The room held its breath. Even the air seemed to still.

Rembran stared at Ixa like a man watching someone drown and being told to let go of the rope.

"I don't know if I can," he whispered.

He didn't see Rana step up beside him, only felt the light brush of her hand at his sleeve.

She hesitated, eyes darting briefly to Rhyslin, then spoke, her voice barely above a breath.

"If you love her," she said, "tell her it's okay to go."

Rembran turned toward her, startled.

"Let her know," she added, "that you'll be here when she comes back."

Her words rang with strange, quiet wisdom, older than her years, anchored in something deeper than training. She hadn't planned to speak. The words had simply risen from her heart.

Rembran stared at her for a long moment.

"When did you get so wise?" he asked, voice thick.

Rana blushed, looking away. "I'm not wise," she murmured. "I just — care."

He leaned down and placed a kiss on her forehead. A silent thank you. Then he turned back toward Ixa.

The world faded around him.

He knelt beside the bench and took her hand, cool and limp in his own.

"Ixa," he whispered, voice catching. "My veiled beauty…"

He bowed his head. His thumb brushed her knuckles.

"Return to *Tir Nan Neoil* with my love. I'll be here when you return, *mo ghraidh.*"

Time held its breath.

Ixa exhaled. Her lips parted faintly as though releasing something sacred.

Her body shimmered, not violently this time, but gently as if made of mist and moonlight. Threads of light unwound from her fingers, her limbs, her hair.

Her form grew translucent… then thinner… then gone.

Only the Ebonwood staff remained, resting where her body had lain.

Rembran reached out and wrapped his fingers around it. The wood was warm and soft with memory. He closed his eyes.

And at that moment, he heard it. A single note, low and strong. Faint, but present. A song with no words, just promise.

Peace washed over him.

He rose slowly and handed the staff to Rhyslin. "I'll catch up with you after we drop your things at the manse," he said, voice calmer now.

He didn't know how long Ixa would be gone. But he would wait.

CHAPTER FIFTEEN

The Ship that Sang to the Wind

The chamber felt hollow without Ixa.

Rhyslin stood still for a breath too long, his staff faintly humming at his side, the sound quieter than usual, like even the magic within it knew to speak softly. The air carried a chill despite the warmth of the stone walls, and for the first time in memory, Rhyslin felt not just tired... but worn. Not bruised. Not strained.

Soul-tired.

He inhaled slowly, letting the air fill his lungs like it might anchor him. He had to change plans. Fast. But first, he had to gather the others.

He turned to Rembran, who was still standing with his head down, one hand curled loosely at his side.

"I know this is a bad time," Rhyslin said gently. "Would you go find Marcus and Sparhawk?"

"Yeah," Rembran murmured, voice hollow. He glanced once at the bench where Ixa had been, then turned to go, shoulders sagging.

Before he could take a step, a hand caught his sleeve.

Rana stood beside him. Her expression was quiet but sure.

"I'll get them," she said, giving his arm a light squeeze. She didn't wait for permission, just turned and slipped through the doorway like a shadow with purpose.

Rhyslin watched her go, one brow faintly raised. A soft pang of pride tugged at his chest.

Then, gathering what remained of himself, he addressed the others.

"There's been a change of plans," he said, glancing across the chamber to a cedar-planked door half-shadowed in the wall. "If you'll follow me." His voice didn't carry command. It didn't need to.

Flur touched Ria's wrist and nodded toward Rowena, who was already turning toward Rembran.

"C'mon," Rowena said, gently catching his hand. "Let's get off our feet."

The group followed Rhyslin in silence.

The hall beyond was quiet. Cool. Candles flickered in old iron sconces, throwing soft golden light across the carved stone. The scent of cedar and parchment drifted faintly from behind the door Rhyslin approached. He paused before it, fingers brushing over the key at his belt.

For a moment, he just breathed.

Then he unlocked the door and pushed it open.

Warm light spilled into the hallway, inviting them in.

The library felt like it had always been waiting for them.

Flur stepped inside first, her golden hair catching the soft lamplight. The room was lined with dark wooden shelves, heavy with books whose spines whispered age and use. A tall window overlooked a garden beyond, letting in the blue-glow haze of early evening. The center of the room was dominated by a long mahogany table ringed with oak chairs.

A crystal sphere floated in the corner, shedding gentle light. The air smelled of beeswax, ink, and old magic.

She ran her fingers through her hair absently as she took it all in. Then, flashing Rhyslin a teasing smile, she swept to the chair beside the head of the table and claimed it.

Her blue eyes twinkled as she leaned back, legs crossed, wholly unrepentant.

Ria entered more slowly.

Her eyes roamed the shelves, widening at the sheer number of books, most of them handwritten, some clearly enchanted.

She wondered if every household in the Saorsa kept such a space or if Rhyslin's was just... special. Her fingers itched to run along the spines.

Instead, she sat beside Flur, her attention drifting toward Rhyslin as he entered last, slower than the others.

He didn't so much sit as he lowered himself into the chair at the table's head, his motions careful, as if his limbs ached deeper than skin and bone. He set his staff beside him with reverent quiet, then leaned back, shoulders heavy with unspoken weight.

Ria reached for him, not aloud, but through their bond. She brushed gently against his thoughts like a whisper in the dark.

{I'm sorry, mo ghraidh. I was trying to —}

{It's okay,} he replied at once, wrapping her in the familiar warmth of his presence. *{I know.}*

{How do you feel?}

He didn't answer immediately. She felt his pause, his resistance to admit it, even to her.

Then, finally:

{Tired.} The word carried layers. Not exhaustion alone, but grief, pressure, and restraint. *{Maybe after this crisis… I can get some rest.}*

Her heart ached. She reached for his hand across the table, holding it without words.

Once Rowena settled with Rembran on her right, Rhyslin lifted his gaze to the gathered faces. The table was full of warmth and quiet concern.

"Before Marcus and Sparhawk get here," he said, voice steady, "I want to explain what's happening."

He relayed the situation, what they'd learned at Saint Ang's Monastery, the shifting plans, the state of the ranges, and his original intent: drop Marcus and Natolie at their home, then return the others to the manse before escorting Rana and Sparhawk's unit to San Ang's.

He paused when Flur raised her hand, her chin tilted with confidence.

"I'm going with you," she said, locking eyes with him. Her tone left no room for negotiation.

Rhyslin exhaled, almost smiling.

"Rana told me you would," he said.

Flur's nod was smug but affectionate. She leaned back in her chair, wholly satisfied.

Rhyslin turned to the others. "What about the two of you?"

Ria pursed her lips in thought. Her heart wanted to follow, but logic held her fast.

"I'm not a fighter," she said at last, her voice soft but sure. "I'll stay at the manse."

She gave him a look, one that burned like fire through their bond.

{You come back. Or I will find you.}

Rhyslin swallowed the knot in his throat and nodded.

{*As will I, mo ghraidh,*} she added through the bond, her voice washing over him like a balm.

{*I'll keep Rowena in line.*}

{*Thank you, my heart,*} he replied.

He let their presence wrap around him, three brilliant, powerful women, each choosing to fight in their own way.

And for the first time in an hour, the fatigue began to lift just a little.

Rhyslin was still basking in the quiet warmth of his bhannan when the door creaked open.

A shadow crossed the threshold, and Marcus leaned in, eyes sweeping the room like a ranger entering a contested glade.

"There you are," he grunted, stepping inside with the ease of a man who had long stopped asking for permission. Behind him came Sparhawk, all quiet edges and sharp-eyed calm, followed closely by Rana, whose braid swung behind her like a trailing whisper of mischief.

Rana brushed past the scout, her pace quick and purposeful. As she reached Rhyslin's side, she claimed the empty chair to his left without hesitation, letting her fingers trail across the wood before she settled in. She waved casually to Sparhawk and patted the chair beside her.

Her pulse, however, was anything but casual.

Sparhawk's slate-gray eyes locked onto hers, steady, unreadable. There was a long beat before he moved, silent as smoke, and took the seat she'd marked for him. Close. Too close.

"Boidhchead le spuirean," he murmured, voice low and rich with unspoken meaning.

Rana's cheeks flushed hot. She looked away quickly, eyes dropping to her lap as her hand curled in her skirt. Her heart thundered in her ears. Why did he make her feel this way? She didn't dare answer until she could speak without stumbling.

Then, still looking down, she whispered, "Fear-fiadhaich le sgaraidhean."

If she'd glanced up, she might've seen the ripple of surprised amusement that passed between Flur and Rowena. Even Marcus's mouth quirked slightly.

At the far end of the table, Ria watched her daughter with narrowed eyes and a slow, growing knot in her chest.

She leaned slightly toward Rhyslin, catching his eye with a single, meaningful arch of her brow.

She's still too young for this, her heart protested.

She didn't voice it. Not yet. But she was already turning over the question she wanted to ask: *Would this man shift the course of the prophecy?* And more importantly, *did Rhyslin know?*

But before she could find the right moment to speak, Rhyslin straightened in his chair and gestured toward Marcus.

"Everything alright?" he asked, voice low but steady.

Marcus shook his head and grunted, "I'm good," firmly anchoring himself beside the door like a sentinel.

"Rana already told us about Ixa," he added, eyes sweeping the table. "What's our move now?"

Rhyslin tapped his fingers once against the wood.

The soft *thok-thok-thok* was the only sound in the library for a beat. Candlelight shimmered off the runes etched into his staff, casting flickering shadows across the table.

Without Ixa, the *Cloud-Dancer* couldn't fly. Which meant...

"We do it the old way," he said. "We gate to the manse, then ride the rest of the way to San Ang's."

Marcus nodded. "That'll work. The kids have our gear squared away. We can be ready to move fast."

Sparhawk spoke next, voice calm but alert. "We can draw from your supply stores. And whatever was already loaded aboard the cutter." He rubbed the edge of his forehead and then glanced at Rana. "Do we have enough horses and wagons?"

Rhyslin considered. "If I don't, the nearest garrison does."

His eyes moved around the table, pausing on each of them in turn, Flur, Ria, Rowena, Rembran, Sparhawk, Rana. No one voiced dissent.

Then, just as he opened his mouth to suggest they move toward the transport chamber,

Knock.

It was sharp. Clear. Unexpected.

The sound cut through the quiet like a blade through silk.

Rhyslin looked toward the door, brows drawing together. He hadn't called for anyone.

Across from him, Marcus had already straightened. The ranger didn't move like he was suspicious but *was ready*. His hand hovered near the hilt of his belt knife as he turned toward Rhyslin and waited.

Rhyslin gave a small nod.

Marcus reached for the handle and cracked the door open to peer out into the council hall beyond.

"Commander Tanner, I'm looking for General Darkblade. Is he in there?"

Marcus's brows lifted slightly. "He is."

"Thank goodness!" the young soldier said with a breath of clear relief. There was an odd lilt in his tone, a formality not meant for Marcus. "There's a lady here trying to find him."

Marcus turned slightly, glancing toward Rhyslin. The draoidh hadn't mentioned expecting anyone. Still, he gave a small nod.

"Very well. Show the lady in, if you please."

"Yes, sir." The soldier turned and stepped back. "He's in here, M'Lady."

Rhyslin's brow lifted the moment he heard the address. *M'Lady?* A ripple of curiosity passed through the room.

Across the table, Flur was already smiling, leaning slightly as if she hoped for a show. Ria's eyes narrowed in quiet speculation.

But it was Rowena who held Rhyslin's gaze, her smile soft, almost knowing like a secret wrapped in velvet.

Then came the voice.

"Thank you, young man."

A moment later, the air in the room shifted. A cool breeze unfurled across the floor, carrying with it the faint, wild scent of high-altitude snow and the hush of distant peaks. Candles flickered. Silence settled like falling frost.

She entered.

Tall, almost as tall as Marcus, and shaped like a willow drawn in moonlight. Her skin was pale as frost-touched quartz, her hair white as snowfall, flowing down her back. A pale, flowing dress clung to her slender frame and pooled around her sandaled feet like a cloud descending. Every step she took was deliberate and graceful, like the breeze had learned to walk.

Rana blinked in open admiration. Even Sparhawk shifted his gaze with mild surprise.

But Rhyslin stood, composed.

The woman's pale blue eyes fell on him, bright with recognition.

"*Lord* Darkblade," she said, a trace of music in her voice. *Ixa was right, his hair is as white as mine>*

"I am Rhyslin Darkblade," he said, offering a polite half-bow. "But I am no lord."

The woman's lashes dipped in apology. "Forgive me. She said you'd deny the title."

"She?" Marcus cut in, arms crossed.

The lady turned toward him and offered a graceful curtsey. "She is Ixa, Master Tanner."

Marcus returned her courtesy with a bow of his own, one brow cocked in amusement. "Does M'Lady have a name?"

She smiled, and for a moment, the whole room seemed to ease around her warmth.

"You may call me Arissa, Lady of the North Wind."

She extended her hand, and Marcus took it, pressing a soft kiss on her knuckles.

"A pleasure, Lady Arissa."

Arissa's grin tilted playfully. "My, my. Such a gentleman."

Her gaze drifted around the room, pausing on each face before settling on Rembran.

"You are Rembran du loch Morn, correct?"

He stood halfway before answering. "I am."

"Good." Her voice gentled, eyes softening as she stepped toward him. "I have a message from Lady Ixa."

Rembran froze. His lips parted, a breath caught in his throat.

"She told me to tell you," Arissa said, her voice almost a caress, "'*I miss you, my love. I will come back to you soon.*'"

Rembran inhaled sharply, the weight of longing breaking through his composure. His shoulders bowed slightly as if from guilt.

"Is she…" his voice cracked. "Is she alright?"

Arissa studied him a moment longer, then let compassion bloom across her features.

"We do not die easily," she said softly. "Lady Ixa will be fine. She merely needs to replenish her mana reserves. She should be able to come back to you in a week."

Rembran closed his eyes. When he opened them, the fear had ebbed, replaced by aching hope.

Rhyslin watched the exchange with quiet approval. Arissa had teased, but only enough to unburden. When her eyes returned to him, he offered a slight incline of his head.

"Lady Arissa," he said. "Did Ixa truly send you all this way just to deliver that message?"

Arissa let out a laugh, bright and effortless.

"Heavens, no!" she replied. "She asked me to assist you until she returns."

She cast a glance toward the others, then added, "She mentioned I'd be working with Ser Andros to fly an airship."

She turned back to Rhyslin, her expression suddenly sharp.

"May I see the ship?"

"Of course," he said, reaching for his staff. As he lifted it over his shoulder, Arissa lifted her hand, fingers trailing a glowing rune through the air. Her gaze flicked from the staff to Rhyslin's chest and back again.

He raised a brow. "Yes?"

Her expression was unreadable, but her voice had gone reverent.

"Do you realize how powerful your prana is?"

A murmur of agreement rippled from his bhannan. Flur made a soft sound of confirmation while Ria tilted her head, eyes studying him anew.

Rhyslin offered a wry shrug. "I've been told it can be felt from stern to bow on the cutter."

Arissa stepped forward, a strand of her silver hair lifting on a breeze that wasn't there.

"They're right," she said. "You and Master Tanner — I felt you both before I even opened the door. You radiate like mountain forges, power shaped, held back, waiting."

Rhyslin tilted his head, measuring her.

"You don't wish to call me Lord. What *do* you prefer?"

She hesitated as if unsure how much familiarity to allow. Then placed her hand over her heart and inclined her head.

"Protocol requires I honor power. Would you accept *Maighstir Darkblade*?"

Rhyslin considered it. She needed formality, for structure, for deference. Not for his sake but her own.

"You may call me that," he said gently. "Or *Maighstir Rhyslin*."

Her eyes widened in horror. "I couldn't," she breathed. "That would be — far too familiar. I don't know you well enough."

The way she clutched her chest was both earnest and amusing.

"We wouldn't want that," Flur murmured playfully to Ria.

A sharp rebuke flicked across the bond, and the golden-haired bhanna lowered her head, cheeks flushing crimson.

Rhyslin let them manage the moment. His attention, however, remained on Arissa, watching her body language, the careful poise with which she spoke and moved. She hadn't truly relaxed since entering. The formality clung to her like a mantle she was unwilling to drop until she knew how tightly the ground beneath her feet held.

"If that's how it must be," he said gently, "you may call me *Maighstir* Darkblade."

Arissa exhaled slightly, the first true easing of her shoulders since her arrival. "Thank you," she said, inclining her head. "I believe you mentioned a ship?"

Rhyslin extended his right hand, slow, open, offering without presumption. No command. Just an invitation.

She paused, assessing the gesture not just with her eyes but with her presence. Once satisfied, she placed her left hand in his.

They stepped outside.

The council chamber faded behind them as a highland breeze brushed past, stirring Arissa's hair. The air was warm for spring, but the wind carried an edge, fresh pine, sun-warmed stone, and a faint scent of sky after rain. The cutter's hull glistened ahead, its oiled sides catching the light like golden bark.

Arissa inhaled deeply. The world here smelled of old trees and drifting ley-lines, alive with quiet magic. She adjusted her sandals and followed Rhyslin across the stone walkway toward the airship.

But just before they reached the stairs, she halted.

"Why does your staff sing praises to He Who Watches?" she asked, voice low and reverent, her gaze drawn toward the black wood resting against his shoulder. "It called to him as though it bore his breath."

Rhyslin glanced at it, his fingers brushing the staff's grain. "Don't all things worship in their own way?" he replied, answering with a question of his own.

That made her pause.

From a few paces back, Flur and Rowena exchanged looks, and even Ria's brow arched in speculative thought.

"You speak," Arissa murmured, "as if you didn't craft it."

"I didn't." Rhyslin's gaze grew distant, his tone softened by memory. "It found me, on the day the oldest Keeper passed beyond the veil. I stepped into the Grove, and it was waiting. Humming with sorrow."

Arissa stilled, hand gently pressed against her chest.

He's one of them, she thought. *One of the true Maighstirean.*

She looked him over again, trying to reconcile his calm bearing with the weight of legend. He didn't seem a day over fifty-five, and yet... that staff was a mark of deeper time.

Her musings scattered when they reached the ship.

"Is this it?" she asked, stopping just short of the gangplank. Her brows lifted slightly.

The *Cloud-Dancer* floated at anchor in the mooring cradle, its hull sleek and narrow, perhaps fifty feet long, with runed plates set into the curvature of the hull. The figurehead was a stylized hawk mid-flight, wings outstretched.

"From what Lady Ixa described," Arissa added, "I expected something larger."

"She was likely thinking of the *Dawn-Breaker*," Rhyslin replied with a small shrug. "She's more familiar with that one. This cutter's newer. Designed for speed and low-profile travel."

Arissa stepped forward, placing her hand against the rail. She closed her eyes.

The ship was young. Restless. Her elemental senses brushed over its pulse; more spirit than memory.

The hull hummed softly under her touch, vibrating with potential but not yet molded by experience.

"She'll fly," Arissa said slowly, "*if* the cargo is properly balanced."

"That's what I hoped to hear," Rhyslin replied, voice easy.

Before he guided her up the gangplank, he turned to her again.

"How often do you need to return to *Tir nan Neoi?*"

"Every four days," she said, holding his gaze. "If I don't return by then, my mana begins to fade, and with it, my ability to maintain form."

She hesitated before adding, "How long until we reach your manse? And from there, the monastery?"

Rhyslin looked skyward. The clouds drifted lazily, not yet heavy with pressure.

"If the winds favor us, we'll be home in a day and a half. From there, another two days to San Ang's."

"Good," she said, nodding. "I should be able to carry you there, but I'll have to return home as soon as we arrive."

Her hands rested on the railing as she glanced up at the mast. "Is the load balanced?"

Rhyslin gave a dry laugh. "We'll find out."

He caught movement near the mid-deck hatch and cupped his hands. "Deck there!"

A sailor's head popped up, freckled, wild-haired, and half-chewing what looked like dried fruit.

"Aye, sir?" he called voice pitching high as he squinted into the sun.

"Send Andros and the cargo master to me."

The sailor snapped a quick salute with fruit-stained fingers and ducked back below.

By the time Arissa joined him near the quarterdeck, a soft wind had picked up. Her hair fluttered like spun silver behind her as she stood beside Rhyslin.

From the dock, Marcus appeared with a wave and vanished down below.

The bhannan, Flur, Ria, and Rowena slipped quietly into the master's cabin, already reacquainting themselves with its space.

Behind them, Rembran and Rana approached the elevated helm.

"Sparhawk's unit is in place and ready to go," Rembran said, more confident now that Arissa's words had uncoiled the knot in his chest.

Rhyslin nodded. "Thank you, Rembran."

Rana stepped beside him, her voice, a breath in his ear. "What are we waiting for?"

Rhyslin smiled faintly, eyes drifting toward the hatch.

"Them."

Two silhouettes began to climb up through the opening, boots thudding softly on the deck, the cutter tilting almost imperceptibly as they stepped aboard.

And the wind, as if sensing what was to come, shifted gently east.

Rana stood near the quarterdeck, a stray lock of dark hair curling across her cheek as the wind picked up. Her gaze followed the two figures emerging from the mid-deck hatch, one steadying the other as they climbed onto the main deck.

The timbers beneath them creaked softly. A hint of lamp oil and fresh pitch drifted in from the rigging lines, mingling with the sharper bite of the highland air.

The man moved with a weighty ease she recognized, a grounding presence that settled the space around him. Her brow lifted. Andros. She hadn't seen him top side yet today, and his appearance reassured her more than she expected. But the woman beside him was unfamiliar.

At her side, Rembran nodded in quiet recognition. "Cargo-mistress Katelyn."

Rana's eyes flicked to him, then back to the woman. Katelyn moved with quiet authority, smoothing the front of her scuffed leather skirt with a callused hand. Her fingers were ink-stained and calloused, used to scrolls and ropes in equal measure. The wind caught her cropped copper-blonde hair, and she tilted her chin as she approached, like someone used to facing gusts head-on.

"Captain," Katelyn greeted cordially, then glanced at the white-haired Elemental standing near the railing. She gave Arissa a once-over and then turned back to business. "Cargo's stowed. I believe the balance is sound, though Lady Ixa would have been more precise." Her voice was brisk, low, and dry like wind over gravel.

She hesitated, then added, "Will she be returning?"

"She will," came a gentle voice. "And I will be joining your crew in the meantime."

Arissa stepped forward, her tone a breeze wrapped in silk. She turned to Andros and offered a graceful nod; palm pressed briefly to her chest. "May the foundation hold you safely, Ser Andros."

The Earth elemental paused mid-step. His eyes, dark as river stone, locked onto hers, and recognition softened the lines around his mouth. "Arissa?" he asked, the name spoken like something half-remembered from a dream.

She extended her hands. "You look different than how I remember."

A faint smile ghosted his face as he took her hands in both of his, holding them with reverent care. "Rembran's mind gave me this form," he said. "I could always change back if..."

"You'll do no such thing," Arissa interrupted, her voice a silken hush. Her fingers tightened slightly around his. "You look so rugged and handsome."

For a heartbeat, something passed between them, old wind and steady stone, mingling like mountain mist over rooted ground. *If I had a heart,* Arissa thought, *it would be dancing like a leaf caught in an updraft.*

Let's Keep in Touch (and in Tales)

I hope you enjoyed reading this book as much as I did writing it.

If you wish to read other books I've written, you will find them, in order, below.

The Draoidh's Cearcall (Series)
1—The Draoidh's Cearcall
2 — The Draoidh's Gambit
3 — The Draoidh's Accord

The Wounded Lands (Series)
1 — The Shadows Rise
2.— The Draoidh's Fall (Forthcoming)
3 — The Withering Range (Forthcoming)

The Law Keeper Chronicles (Series)
1 — The Black Swan's Bond
2 — The Sheriff's Oath
3 — By Law and Flame

The House of Healing (Series)
1 — Oath & Ember
2 — The Living Grove
3 — The Draoidh's Return

If you want to tag along for the fun, join my mailing list at: https://josephwiess.substack.com/

Or you can come to my author page at https://joseph-l-wiess-author.com/

www.ingramcontent.com/pod-product-compliance
Lightning Source LLC
Chambersburg PA
CBHW071453140726
47997CB00005B/1707